# Soul Screams

## Sara Jayne Townsend

ISBN: 978-0-9530016-2-0

Published by Stumar Press 2012.

www.stumarpress.co.uk

First published in Great Britain by Stumar Press 2012.

ISBN: 978-0-9530016-2-0.

British Library Cataloguing in Publication Data. A catalogue for this book is available from the British Library.

# Dedication

Real friends are hard to find. Real friends know you well and love you anyway.

This book is dedicated to Tanya Burley and Angela Sandwith Bruce.

Real friends.

# Acknowledgements

Some of these stories go back a long way. I'd like to thank, first and foremost, the T Party Writers' Group, which in its 18-year history has seen many of these stories, in one form or another, and helped me whip them into shape. Special thanks to Sarah Ellender and Gaie Sebold, who are always there when I want to complain about writing and life in general over a glass of wine.

Some of the stories in this collection pre-date the T Party. Writing has played a big part in keeping me sane over the years, but my friends have played an even bigger role. I don't choose friends easily, or lightly. Those I do choose, I choose for life. Friends have provided inspiration and a lifeline over the years. Some of them have inspired stories, as mentioned in the Postscripts. Others I have dedicated this collection to.

So I'd like to thank all of the other significant friends in my life I have not yet mentioned. The friends who used to put up with me hanging around with them in high school – Kathryn Thomsen, Anita Redwood, Mark Lasso and Laura Wright. They always said they were looking forward to the day when they could say, "I knew her before she was famous, you know". They're still waiting for that day – but I have no doubt they are all going to buy this book. I also want to say thank you to Jay Thiessen, who helped me survive Grade 8 and who I still consider a friend.

Thank you – again – to Aaron Solomon and Andrea Cleary. You've always liked me for who I am. Even when I was the geeky smart kid that nobody else liked. We were the original Trio.

Thank you to Paul Bruce, Richard Burley, Luke Thomas and David Gullen – friends in their own right, but who also deserve extra credit for putting up with the absence of their partners when I am most in need of girly chats.

And finally, thank you to Ayo Onatade and Kirstie Long. I can always rely on you to provide honest and frank advice. And a bottle of wine.

*Cigarette Burns* first published in *Grotesque* (1994).

*Jimi Hendrix Eyes* first published in *Peeping Tom* (1998) and subsequently in *Deep Ten* (2004) and *Kiss The Sky* (2007).

*Just Don't Scream* first published in *Peeping Tom* (1991).

*Kay's Blues* first published in *Roadworks* (2002).

*Morgan's Father* first published in *Roadworks* (2000).

*Road To Maladomini* first published in *Sierra Heaven* (1998).

*The Thirteenth Floor* first published as *The Top Floor* in *FEAR* (1989).

*Trio* first published in *Gravity's Angels* (1998).

*Someone To Watch Over You*, *The Boy With Blue Eyes*, *The Guitar*, *The Wedding Hat* and *To Dream of An Angel* are all published for the first time in *Soul Screams* (2012).

# Contents

# Foreword

It's gratifying to come across yet another writer such as Sara Jayne Townsend who, rather than stay safely within the various genre 'boxes' beloved of many agents and publishers, has shifted and merged the perceived parameters of crime, the paranormal and horror so very effectively in her impressive first collection of short stories. The powerful title perfectly suggests what's in the tin. Those domains beyond our earthly existence, and deep complexities of the human mind. In this collection, the crimes of which we are all capable, aren't merely depicted as whodunnits, but *why*dunnits. I feel a complete empathy with what she has achieved – a balanced yet ultimately disturbing and thought-provoking read.

To me, the most frightening scenarios lie close to home; to the everyday, and in her first story, *The Thirteenth Floor*, Paul sets off to spend Halloween with Tony in his flat. So far so normal, until Townsend, to her immense credit, gradually and believably, ratchets up the horror of the past impinging upon the present. Not only that, but I was also left fearful for the future. A strong sense of claustrophobia pervades not only the apartments themselves but also a terrible history.

I was reminded of Koji Suzuki's short story collection, *Dark Water*, where what lurks beneath the everyday in sanitised Japan, is skilfully exposed. Like him, Townsend has created characters I cared about. Not a cardboard cut-out in sight, which made their feelings, actions and their fates all the more startling.

Townsend's brave imagination doesn't shy away from touches of humour, as in *Kay's Blues* the eponymous main character describes her period pain as feeling like "a dwarf swinging from your kidneys". Yet in *To Dream of An Angel* the tone becomes quite profound, where "dreams are fragments of a past reality – half-remembered details from a former incarnation".

Just a morsel from an intriguing story that – being a serial dreamer – has lodged in my mind. As has that eerily glowing guitar in *The Guitar* and the subject of *The Wedding Hat* with its unconventional saleswoman.

There's something of the Surrealists in the imagery here too, especially that of René Magritte with his inventive twists on 'reality'. The vivid scenes Townsend creates are solid enough but laced with an other-worldly ambiguity. Although I wasn't always clear exactly where, geographically these strange events happen, this didn't detract from my complete immersion into this author's worlds where voices are real, with a contemporary edge, surely adding to this collection's appeal. However, anyone expecting a calm crossing will be in for a surprise. Townsend's own dark waters are churning with passionate life. And death.

From *Morgan's Father* and its shocking ending to *The Boy With Blue Eyes* whose cruel beauty ensnares with growing danger, his innocent admirer. From the aptly titled, *Just Don't Scream* where a fairground adventure becomes a dice with death, to the deeply chilling *Cigarette Burns*, this particular ocean is not for the unwary.

Keep a lifebelt handy. Keep the light on ...

So, with my blood considerably cooler and my nerves on high alert, I arrived at *Someone To Watch Over You*, the story to end the journey. From beyond the grave, Elizabeth Anne Beresford possesses the uncanny power to not only observe but manipulate the lives of those close to her. To haunting effect. Which is how I'd sum up my immediate and still lingering response to *Soul Screams*.

I have been haunted.

A rare achievement from a writer who is proving she's someone to watch. The next Stephen King? You might ask. It's more than possible.

## *Sally Spedding*
Crime Mystery Author
www.sallyspedding.com

# Introduction

I never know how to answer the question, "when did you know you wanted to be a writer?" For me the answer is, since always. I have been writing stories since the time I learned how to write. Even before then, I was making up stories – as a child I had an array of dolls and soft toys. They all had individual names, personalities and family histories. Every night I'd select one to take to bed with me, making up a story featuring that toy as the central character before I was able to sleep at night.

I am a writer. I didn't choose to be so, anymore than I chose to be left-handed or have green eyes. The writing has been with me since the beginning, and in so many ways it's been an outlet. Every time I've had trouble coping with difficult feelings or emotions, writing a story about these feelings has helped me cope with them. Certain themes crop up a lot, especially in my early work. Betrayal. Loneliness. Isolation. Death. These are all fears and insecurities that I've tried to deal with at some point in life. My dearly departed grandmother, bless her, used to disapprove of the subject matter of my stories. "Why can't you write more cheerful stories?" she would ask, every time she'd finished reading the latest offering in which someone else meets a miserable and gruesome death. The answer is because happy feelings I want to hold on to. The negative feelings I try to exorcise, and they end up in my stories.

There is a myth – possibly perpetuated by Freud – that all writers are mad. I think maybe the opposite is true. Writers are just that little bit more sane than everyone else, because we have an outlet for the insanity. Commuting everyday on a crowded London underground train, nose pushed into someone else's armpit, can drive a person mad. But though I am often tempted to mow down everyone in the carriage, after just one more inexplicable delay, I'm never going to snap and do it for real. I'll go away and write about that frustration instead.

Hopefully you've not come to this collection expecting some uplifting stories, because that isn't what they are all about. I chose the title *Soul Screams* because it seemed very appropriate. All these stories are about that inner scream that no one can hear but you.

This journey you are about to undertake might be a bumpy one. But I'd like to thank you for getting on board with me. Writing can be a lonely business. It always helps to know there's someone else coming along for the ride.

Sara Jayne Townsend

Carshalton

March 2012

# The Thirteenth Floor

I sniggered uncontrollably. I couldn't help it.

"What's so funny?" Tony asked.

"You are, Tony old pal," I replied. We were sitting in the well-worn armchairs of my parents' living room when he broke his momentous news.

"I'm serious, Paul."

"Yeah, right. You? Moving out?"

"You don't believe me?" Tony adopted a wounded tone.

"Tony, you and me have been friends for how long now? Ten years? You've never done the shopping, you've never done the laundry, the only thing you've ever cooked is beans on toast. How are you going to manage without your mum around to do these things for you?"

Tony shrugged. "I just decided I need my own space. It's time to get some independence."

"I bet twenty quid you won't last a week."

Tony stuck out his hand. "Alright, mate, you're on. Twenty quid."

After a moment's hesitation, I duly shook on it. "You're really serious about this, aren't you?"

"Yeah, I am serious. In fact, I've already found somewhere."

"Oh yeah? Where?"

"A flat in a tower block, on the other side of town. A bit out of the way, I suppose, but it suits me, and it's the right price. I've already signed the papers. I move in on October the 15th."

"I still think you'll be back home inside of a week with a bag full of laundry, begging your mum for a decent meal."

Tony smiled. "We'll just see," he said.

*

I lost my twenty quid. Tony phoned me a week and a half after he moved in. "Why don't you come and see the place for yourself?" he said. "You can bring round my winnings while you're at it. Come round on Friday. I'll get some beer in and a takeaway, maybe a DVD."

I agreed. I was curious to see Tony's flat. He'd been pretty secretive about it so far.

Friday was Halloween. After work I went home to change, and then headed straight for Tony's. Two boys approached me as I walked to my car and yelled, "trick or treat!" One of them was wearing a black cloak and a mask like the character from 'Scream'. The other wore an alien mask. Since I had no sweets on me, I gave them each a pound and reflected on the growing phenomena of trick-or-treating as I got into my car. I knew it was hugely popular in the States, but it appeared to be picking up over here, too.

I looked again at the directions Tony had given me over the phone as I set off. I didn't recognise too many of the street names. I had lived in Bellingford all twenty-two years of my life. It wasn't a very big place, yet when I turned off Caroline Street I found myself completely lost.

Eventually, diligently following Tony's directions, I thought I had reached the right place. I found myself in front of an old and nondescript tower block of flats, part of a small estate comprised of shabby buildings and tiny alleyways. The estate was hidden among the trees just off a quiet country road that didn't seem to be part of Bellingford at all.

I parked my fifteen-year-old Ford Escort in the pot-holed car park and sat there for a minute, gazing up at the building and wondering why in hell Tony had taken a fancy to such a depressing-looking place. I suspected it was all he could afford; even renting property was expensive these days. The building towered twelve or thirteen floors, brown and dirty and neglected. Uniform windows crawled up each side in parallel lines, behind which could be seen grey curtains or dusty Venetian blinds. A row of balconies ran vertically up the side of one wall, painted in a shade of cream which had faded over the years. All the balconies sported rusty spots, and most of them had a line of washing stretched across them. I cursed under my breath as I stared at the building. I knew Tony was on a tight budget, as I was, but even so, I couldn't imagine why he would prefer living here to his mum's house.

I climbed out of my car with a six-pack of Budweiser, and made sure all the doors were locked before walking over to the building. Everything was eerily quiet. If I strained I could just about make out the roar of traffic on the motorway in the distance, but apart from that I could hear nothing. It was just after six, but it was already dark. The air was damp, the kind of dampness that only comes with British winters, a dampness that permeates your flesh and chills you down to the very bones. I turned up my collar against the October night, and hurried on.

As I reached the lobby I saw a woman with a pram and two young children struggling to get through the front door. She was overweight, with stringy hair, wearing black leggings and an oversize blue shirt. I held the door open for her, and she thanked me with a mumbled "Ta, love" as she manoeuvred pram and kids outside. I'd taken her to be middle-aged at first, but as she passed me I got a closer look at her face and saw she was much younger – probably not much older than me.

Finding myself in the lobby of the building, I let the door fall shut and walked over to the lift. I pressed the button, but the light in the centre did not come on. Then I noticed a piece of paper taped to the wall. On it someone had written: 'LIFT OUT OF ORDER.' The tape that held the sign to the wall was yellowing. I wondered how long the lift had been out of order, and how many safety regulations the landlord was breaking by not getting it fixed. Resignedly I tramped over the faded red carpet towards the stairwell.

The doors of the individual flats were dark brown rectangular stains in walls painted off-white – or perhaps they had been painted white, and had faded over years to the dull colour they were now. Looking closer, it seemed more likely that years of nicotine absorption had coloured the walls this shade. Cigarette burns in the nylon carpet further belied the fact that many smokers had passed along here for years before the smoking ban had been enforced.

The building was completely silent. A phrase from some school text or another drifted into my head: 'The silence was deafening.' I had never paid much attention to that particular phrase before – to be honest, I hadn't paid much attention in school to anything – but now it seemed disturbingly appropriate. The silence in the corridor was so overpowering, it drowned out everything else.

I reached the door at the end of the corridor. An exit sign flickered above it, the lights behind it faulty. I pushed open the door and began climbing up the stairs to the ninth floor.

By the time I reached Tony's door – flat 912 – I had not seen or heard anyone since the woman in the lobby, and this made me uneasy. Surely I should have heard a radio, sounds of a Halloween party, seen somebody on their way out to the pub, or some kids in Halloween costumes wandering around? But there was nothing.

I raised my fist and rapped on Tony's door. The noise resounded through the too-quiet corridor. I shivered involuntarily. "Dammit, Tony, where are you?"

I knocked again and stared at the door, willing it to open. I fumbled in my jacket pocket for the piece of paper on which I had written Tony's address and directions. Flat 912, he had told me. This was the right building, and the right door. He knew I was coming. So where the hell was he?

I was beginning to feel like an idiot standing there in the corridor staring at a door, and my arms were beginning to ache from carrying the beer. I was just thinking about going back to my car and drinking a can or two while I waited, when I heard a female voice call out. It was very clear, and distinctly said, "Paul!"

I whirled around, startled by the sudden noise, and saw a girl walking down the corridor towards me. She was small, a bit on the thin side, but with very long legs, which were encased in a tight pair of jeans. She moved gracefully, almost seeming to float rather than walk. She had pale blonde hair that hung limply to her shoulders, and looked about nineteen. She was smiling at me, as though she recognised me. I tried desperately to think if this was someone I knew, but I could not recall ever seeing her before.

"Er ... hello," I said awkwardly.

"Hello," she said. "What's up?" She stopped about a foot away and gazed at me intently. Her eyes fascinated me. They were a very light blue, and had a dullness about them. Her face was unhealthily pale.

"Er, my friend." I gestured vaguely at the door. "He invited me round, but he doesn't seem to be in."

"I'm sure he won't be gone long," the girl said. She was still staring at me, and I could feel faint beads of sweat breaking out on my forehead. It was as if she could see right into my soul. "But if you don't want to wait out here in the hall, you can always come up to my flat for a while. Oh, my parents are home," she added quickly.

I blinked and stepped back, not sure whether I was more surprised at the sudden invitation, or the fact that she seemed to have picked up on the rather unpious thought that had crossed my mind when she issued it.

"My brother came home today you see and ..." she trailed off uncertainly. "If you'd rather not, that's alright."

"Well, it's just that Tony'll probably be here any minute, and I should wait here, so he knows where I am," I mumbled self-consciously.

She shrugged. "Well, if you change your mind, you know where to find me. See you later, Paul." She headed towards the stairs.

I called after her. "Wait!"

She paused and turned around.

"Where can I find you?" I asked.

The smile she gave me lit up her face, and for just a moment she was the most beautiful girl I had ever seen. "The top floor, of course," she said sweetly.

I watched her as she opened the door at the end of corridor and disappeared up the stairs. Then, after a moment's hesitation, I went after her. To this day, I'm not exactly sure why.

I started to climb the stairs. I couldn't see the girl above me, but she had said the top floor, so that's where I was going. As I passed the door for the twelfth floor, I wondered just how many floors this building had. The building hadn't looked much higher than twelve stories from the outside – but then again, I thought, things aren't always what they seem.

I swung around the corner and started up the next set of steps. My trainers made a dull thud on the strip of grooved rubber that covered the metal steps. A few steps from the top, my foot caught in a hole in the rubber and I stumbled, catching hold of the banister to keep my balance. At the top of this set of steps the stairwell ended at a door flaked with peeling grey paint. Large plastic characters displayed the number '13'. The three had come loose and hung at a skewed angle.

I reached out to put my hand on the metal handle. As I touched it, I had a sensation like a mild electrical charge coursing through my body. I drew my hand away quickly. After a moment, I reached out and touched the handle again, very carefully. Nothing. Uneasily, I opened the door.

I stepped into the corridor, carefully. Step by cautious step I moved forward, almost afraid of disturbing the dead silence.

Suddenly the air was split by a terrified scream, and I stopped dead. I stood frozen for a split second, uncertain whether to help whoever was in trouble, or run like hell.

The scream came again, from a door to my left. Just as I registered the source of the scream, the door flew open. The girl I had encountered downstairs clutched desperately at the doorjamb, her pale eyes wide with terror. Behind her, a hulking figure loomed, a tall heavy-set man with wild tousled hair. He looked like a young man apart from his eyes, which seemed to hold the soul of someone startlingly old.

"Paul!" the girl screamed. "Help me!" Please!" She reached clawed fingers out to me. The man behind her had one heavily-muscled arm clamped around her waist. He slammed her roughly against the doorframe. Her head banged the wood of the frame and she screamed again, staring at me in terror. The two of them remained framed in the doorway for a split second, the girl helplessly caught and struggling, her captor wearing a look of maniacal fury. His free arm was raised above his head. In his hand he clutched a bloodied axe.

I remained rooted to the spot, unable to do anything but watch in helpless terror. What happened next happened so quickly I would not have been able to do anything to stop it, even if I had been able to move. The man released the girl momentarily, clutched the axe in both his hands, and swung it with such force the cords in his arms strained with the effort. The axe cleaved effortlessly through the girl's neck and embedded itself in the doorframe. The girl's body dropped unceremoniously to the floor. Her head hit the ground with a sickening thud and rolled towards me, coming to rest with the dead eyes staring up at me in terror, the lips parted forever in an eternal scream.

I stepped back in horror and stumbled over something on the floor. I turned and stared in disbelief at the sight which met my eyes. Partial bodies and limbs were scattered all over the hallway, a sea of blood spreading slowly across the carpet, flowing down the walls.

I heard the killer roar with anger, and I turned around. The man grabbed the axe with both hands and pulled it free of the frame where it had become stuck. Then he raised the axe above his head, and turned to stare at me. As he took a first thundering step towards me, I found the power to break free of my paralysis. I turned and fled down the hallway, back towards the stairs, dropping the beer in my panic.

I took the stairs two at a time, half-running, half-falling all the way down to the ground floor. I never looked back to see whether or not I was being followed.

At the bottom of the stairs I tore along the ground floor corridor. I screeched to a halt in front of the lift where Tony stood, a Sainsbury's plastic bag in each hand. "Tony! Where the hell have you been?"

He looked at me in surprise. "I just drove a friend to the supermarket because her car's broken down. Hey man, sorry I wasn't here when you got here. Say, what's with you? You look like you've seen a ghost."

"Something a lot worse." I grabbed my friend's arm. "We've got to call the police. There's a nutcase up on the thirteenth floor, killing people. There are bodies everywhere."

Tony was staring at me with an odd look on his face. "What are you talking about? We don't have a thirteenth floor."

"I was just up there. I saw him hack a girl's head off." I leaned against the wall to catch my breath, my heart hammering against my ribs. "I just ran all the way down."

"Paul, this building's only got twelve floors." The lift door slid open as Tony spoke.

I stared at him. "I thought the lift was broken."

"It's very temperamental, but today it's working. No worries." Tony stepped into the lift. "Come on, man, let's go."

"But ..." I pointed to the sign pasted to the wall outside the lift.

"Oh, that. The goddamn thing breaks down so often the landlord never bothers taking the sign down." Tony put down one of his grocery bags and stabbed at the 'door open' button. The doors stopped sliding closed and opened again. "Come in here and look at these buttons. The last one is twelve."

I stepped into the lift and peered at the panel. The panel in the wall featured an ordinary row of lift buttons. The bottom one said 'G', the next one up '1', and so on all the way up to '12'. There was nothing above twelve.

"I tell you, I was up there. There's a killer up there."

"Maybe you got the floors mixed up. We should check it out." Tony pressed '12'. The lift doors slid shut.

"He might still be up there. We should call the cops."

"We should check it out first," Tony said.

"What, you don't believe me? You think I'm imagining things?"

"I never said that, Paul. I just want to check it out myself, that's all."

I said nothing. The lift seemed to close in as it made its ascent. I watched the numbers go by on the display. '4. 5. 6.'

Time was standing still, each number lingering for an eternity before moving to the next. '7. 8. 9.' The lift seemed to be getting smaller.

As the display reached '12', the lift stopped moving. The doors opened.

I was rooted to the spot, fear washing over me. Tony was already out of the lift, looking up and down the corridor. He looked back at me, a puzzled look on his face. He still held the grocery bags, one in each hand.

I got out cautiously and looked around. The corridor was as silent and empty as a school in the middle of August. "Tony, it was the thirteenth floor. Not the twelfth."

"And I'm telling you there is no thirteenth floor. This is as far as the lift goes. There's nothing else. Now can we go back downstairs and drop off these goddamn bags before the bottoms fall out of them?"

But I was already running towards the stairs. I banged open the fire door that led to the stairwell. I looked up at the steps going up. "Tony, look there." Tony came up behind me, muttering furiously. I pointed to a step halfway up. "See there, the rubber lining is torn. I remember that. I came up these steps and I tripped there. Just after that I came out onto the thirteenth floor."

"Paul, those stairs go nowhere," Tony called after me. I climbed determinedly up the stairs and stopped short at a blank wall.

I stared in disbelief at the peeling paint. I reached out and touched the wall, still believing that it wasn't really there, that it would dissolve away to reveal the carnage that lay behind it. The wall was hard, cold concrete. I continued staring at it. The wall remained blank, solid and unmoving.

"Paul," Tony said gently.

"I'm telling you, it was here," I shouted angrily. "There was a door. I went through it. A man with an axe chased me, and then I ran all the way back down to the ground floor."

"Paul," Tony said after a pause, "you haven't … you haven't been … taking anything?"

I suddenly understood. "Oh come on, I've not touched that stuff for years. I've been clean for a long time now, you know that."

"Well yeah, but …" he trailed off uncertainly.

I was furious. Furious at my friend, for even suggesting such a thing, furious at the door that suddenly, mysteriously wasn't there, furious at the part of myself that doubted it had ever been there in the first place. "Goddammit, Tony, you're supposed to be my friend. I thought you knew me better than that."

Tony turned away. "Look …" Clearly having difficulty choosing words, he changed the subject. "Carrie's gonna be wondering where her shopping is. Let's get rid of this stuff."

Tony headed back to the lift, and we travelled in silence down to the fifth floor. He didn't look at me, choosing instead to study the floor while we waited in the lift.

We walked without speaking down the fifth floor corridor, approaching a small, dark-haired woman who peered out of the open door of flat 502. She looked older than us; I pegged her to be in her late twenties. I knew Tony was attracted to petite brunettes, so I assumed he probably fancied her. He hadn't said anything about a new girlfriend, though.

"I thought you were right behind me," the woman said to Tony.

"Sorry, Carrie. I ran into Paul downstairs. Paul, meet Carrie. A friend of mine."

Tony still avoided looking me in the eye, and escaped into the flat. I offered my hand for Carrie to shake. "Hi," I said.

"Hi Paul," she said. As she shook my hand she looked at me with a strange expression on her face and something like recognition flickered for a moment in her eyes. Then it was gone, and she was smiling at me. "Pleased to meet you. I hope you weren't waiting too long. Tony very kindly offered to drive me to Sainsbury's after I spent half an hour trying to get my car to start."

"Carrie!" Tony hollered from inside the flat. "Where do you want all this stuff?"

"Excuse me." Carrie smiled and gestured to the lounge. "Please, make yourself comfortable. I just have to liberate my groceries from Tony, and we'll be right with you."

I wandered into the other room, which was small but cosy. The far wall contained a French window leading out to the balcony, hung with floral print curtains. Another wall finished at a hallway which I presumed led out to the bathroom and bedrooms. There was a bookcase and a set of shelves on a third wall.

I walked past the bookcase, idly looking at things on it while I waited. As well as books – mostly non-fiction large hardback books, dealing with such things as aircraft of the Second World War, history, and the paranormal, there were a few china ornaments and two framed photographs. One A4 size picture, in a brass frame, was of Carrie looking resplendent in a wedding dress, arm in arm with a tall, dark-haired man who was grinning broadly. Carrie was married, then. The decor seemed to indicate a man lived here as well as a woman (and I assumed the aircraft books were his, too), though I hadn't seen any sign of Carrie's husband being at home.

The other picture was smaller and older. In this photo a teenaged Carrie stood beaming in a red mini dress. Beside her stood another girl in a yellow dress. She looked healthier and happier than she had done when I had seen her, but there was no doubt that this girl in the photo was the one I had encountered in the corridor not half an hour earlier. I grabbed the picture and stared at it.

Tony and Carrie swept into the room. "Carrie and her husband helped me move in," Tony said. "They've been really good."

"The kettle's on," said Carrie. "Paul, do you want tea or coffee?"

I handed Carrie the photograph. "Who's this in this photo?"

Carrie looked at it and smiled sadly. "That's me and my best friend Lisa Killan. On the night of her seventeenth birthday party."

"Tony, that's her. That's the girl I saw."

Tony sighed. "Paul ..."

I turned to Carrie. "When I first arrived, and Tony was out, I was standing outside his flat and this girl came up to me. This girl in the picture. I was standing there, and she told me she lived on the top floor, and then she started going up the stairs, and I followed her all the way up and came out on the thirteenth floor. Then I heard screams, and I saw this big bastard with an axe drag her out of a flat, and he cut off her head. There was blood everywhere, bodies all over the place. Then the killer came after me, and I ran all the way downstairs and ran into Tony in the lobby."

"But we went upstairs. There is no thirteenth floor, I showed you that," Tony protested. "Hey Carrie, are you okay?"

Carrie's face was ashen. She sank down in the sofa. For a long time she said nothing. Tony and I just stared at her. When she did finally speak, her voice was very soft. "I moved into this building as a child, with my parents. There was a thirteenth floor then."

Tony stared at her. "What?"

"Lisa was my best friend at school." Carrie went on as if she hadn't heard him. "She lived on the thirteenth floor, with her mother and siblings. They were quite a poor family. She had two younger sisters and a baby brother. There was also an older brother, who had a very violent temper. He was committed to a mental asylum after he attacked one of his teachers and put her in hospital. I don't know what was wrong with him, but he was unstable and very dangerous. He was away for about eight years, and then they said he had had treatment, and he was a lot better, a lot calmer, and he was allowed home. Lisa told me it was initially just for a long weekend, so they could see how he was at home. If all went well, he would be allowed to stay at home.

"I don't know what happened during that time. Something made him snap, I don't know what. But he wasn't better. During that weekend visit he slaughtered his entire family. The building had axes hung near the fire doors in those days, with the fire extinguishers, you know for emergencies, if there was a fire and you had to smash open the door to get out. David stole one of them and hacked his family to pieces. Mother, brother, sisters ... including Lisa. I didn't see the bodies. The ambulance came, there were police everywhere, and David was taken away again. I found out later that Lisa had been decapitated.

"After that, everyone who lived on the thirteenth floor moved out, and a decision was made to close off the floor. I don't suppose they ever managed to get rid of all the blood. But the building's had twelve floors ever since. Most people who lived here then have moved away, so none of the current residents know about what happened that terrible day. No one talks about it. I don't really know why I stayed. By the time I married Graham, Dad was dead, Mum was ill, and we didn't have much money, so we moved in with Mum to look after her. Then when she died we just didn't bother moving out. I guess I grew attached to this flat. I've lived here all my life. I feel that I can still be close to Lisa here – close to the good memories, rather than remembering the terrible way she died." Carrie paused. "It all sounds so clichéd, like a bad horror film. The thirteenth floor, Halloween, deranged killer, and all that. But that was how it happened."

She looked up at us. "Today's Halloween, isn't it? That's the day it happened. Friday, October thirty-first, nineteen ninety-six. Twelve years ago today."

"This is nuts," I muttered furiously.

"There's something else." Carrie still gazed up at Tony and me. We fell silent, waiting for her to continue. "Lisa's boyfriend was killed that day, too. It seems he arrived just in time for David's killing spree."

Carrie rose and crossed over to the bookcase. She pulled a photograph album from one of the lower shelves. She returned to the sofa and flipped through the pages. "Here. This is a picture of him. Lisa's boyfriend."

Tony and I leaned over Carrie's shoulders to look at the photo to which she was pointing. It was of a young man straddling an amusement park dinosaur. The clothes belonged to a previous decade, and his hair was longer and slightly lighter, but the resemblance between his face and mine was uncanny. He could have been my brother.

Tony looked at the picture, and then stared at me. "It's ... it's unreal," he stammered.

"The resemblance struck me when I met you, but I thought it was just coincidence until you told your story." Carrie looked up at me sadly. "But that's not all. His name was Paul, too. Paul Thompson. He was twenty-one when he was killed."

"Jesus Christ." I sank onto the sofa as the terrible truth sank in. "Ghosts? Twelve-year-old murders replaying themselves on a floor that doesn't exist? A man that looked like me, with my name? What the hell does it all mean?"

We sat in silence on the sofa, the three of us. The room suddenly felt oppressive and enclosed, filled with the wraiths of a violent past. It was Carrie who broke the silence, and her words lingered in the air long after she had spoken them.

"I don't know."

# Jimi Hendrix Eyes

"A lot depends on your attitude," Lisa said. "Guys have a fundamentally different attitude to sex than girls, don't they?"

"Some do, I guess," I said carefully.

"That's why I've never talked about sex with you," she went on. She sat on the sofa, feet curled under her, wearing tracksuit bottoms, baggy T-shirt and fluffy socks. She looked very childish, I thought. "In ... how many years have we known each other? We talk about everything else. I can talk to you more easily than my girl friends. But you're a guy, so you'll have different opinions about sex. So we don't talk about it."

I wasn't sure she was right, and didn't reply. The argument didn't seem right to me, and I reckoned it was more the wine making her say those things than anything else. The empty bottle had been unopened two hours ago. Lisa's cheeks were flushed and her blonde hair was mussed, falling untidily over her face.

"I was a virgin when I met Michael. You didn't know that, did you?"

"No," I replied simply. It didn't surprise me really; she was looking at me as though she thought it should. We'd been friends for a very long time; we had gone our separate ways at college, to a certain degree – mingled with different crowds, developed separate interests – but still remained close enough to talk to each other about our romantic interests. Lisa hadn't had that many boyfriends, but she'd dated a few guys regularly. When Michael came along it had been different; the transformation in her had been incredible. She seemed to almost physically glow; the happiness she radiated was so powerful. It had been wonderful to see her like that. She told me she at last knew what real love was, and she and Michael moved in together within six months of meeting each other.

"I wanted to wait for the right person," Lisa said. "I wanted it to be special. Sex should be special. It should be an expression of love, a bond between two people who care deeply about each other. What sense is there in sex just for the sake of sex? Most men don't seem to understand that. They want the grope, the orgasm. No tenderness, no affection, no love. Michael's different. He wanted to wait, too. When we found each other we knew we were right for each other."

"But I understand," I said. I was not surprised at Lisa's revelation because I knew her. I knew she wanted to wait for sex to be special because I could understand that myself. There were so many things I wanted to say, but I couldn't find the words. In the end nothing else needed to be said. Lisa sat watching me, pushing the hair out of her eyes. The empty wine bottle stood on Michael's amplifier, which doubled as a coffee table, beside the sofa.

Something passed between us, silent and invisible, and I knew then that our fate was to be sealed that night. Maybe it can be traced back even further. Maybe to the day we met, whenever and wherever that was. I could never remember exactly, only that Lisa had always been there, had always been my best friend. Maybe that action of meeting had set in motion the cycle that was to destroy three lives. I had loved Lisa all the time I had known her, and somewhere deep inside me, perhaps I had always known that I longed to love her physically and she felt the same for me, and that one day it would surface. But for all these years, that knowledge had been suppressed, smothered, as if I had also known that if it were to happen it would be a terrible thing.

So Lisa and I had gone on being friends all this time, able to read each other's minds, able to understand each other's very thoughts, able to talk to each other about absolutely anything except the one thing we really wanted to talk about. That was the real reason we had never discussed sex. The night we did the die was cast, and the thing that had been fated to happen from the beginning could be held back no longer.

Lisa spoke not another word to me, and held out her hand. I went to her, kneeling on the floor in front of the sofa. I took her outstretched hand. She leaned forward, her face close to mine. I stroked her hair with my other hand, cupped the side of her face, bringing her closer to me, and our lips found each other.

I had never kissed Lisa before, not even given her a peck on the cheek, and had never even allowed myself to think I might want to, but somewhere in the back of my mind I had played the scene out over and over again. The press of her lips, the taste of her skin, seemed familiar to me, memories of a long-suppressed desire. It was as if a valve had been opened, and years of pent-up emotion came flooding out in a torrent. Lisa's hands were at the back of my head, holding me close to her. The touch of her hand in my hair was sending shivers down my spine. I ran my hand down the side of her neck, over the swell of her breast, across her abdomen, finding the bottom of her T-shirt and fumbling for the soft flesh beneath it.

Lisa's hand found mine and removed it, and for a terrifying moment I thought I had somehow been reading it all wrong – until I looked into her eyes, and saw all the answers there. She stood up, raising me up with her. Holding my hand, she walked backwards towards the bedroom, her eyes never leaving mine.

We never spoke another word to each other that night. There was nothing else that needed to be said. Clumsily we undressed each other, clothes piling up in an untidy heap on the floor. We made love that night in her bed, in the bed she shared with Michael. Never before had I felt such fulfilment in lovemaking, never had I experienced such a feeling of oneness, of giving so willingly and taking so gratefully. And all the while we had Michael's clock radio flashing red digits at us, Michael's science fiction paperbacks piled up on the bedside table beside us, Michael's Jimi Hendrix poster on the wall watching everything we did, witness to the ultimate betrayal.

What hurt most was the fact that Michael was genuinely my friend. I had met all the men Lisa had gone out with for any length of time; some of them didn't mind her friendship with me, some did. None of them had accepted me as well as Michael did. He had never minded Lisa and me going out alone – he trusted both of us implicitly. Michael worked as a rep for a computer software company, and was often away overnight. Rather than getting jealous about her spending so many evenings with me when he was away, he was glad that she had some company. Michael and I had a common interest in music – he played guitar and I played bass – and we got together frequently for jamming sessions. His most treasured possession was his extensive collection of record albums, nearly a thousand in all, which he had spent fifteen years building up. He and Lisa had had to go for a flat with a second bedroom when they were getting their place together, so they would have room for all the records. They were all stored in the spare bedroom, stacked up in boxes from floor to ceiling, all neatly arranged in alphabetical order from AC/DC to ZZ Top. There was nothing in the world that Michael cared about more than his record collection. Except Lisa.

I lay awake most of the night, in Michael's half of the bed, while Lisa slept. Jimi Hendrix gazed down at me. The camera had caught him straight on for the picture, posed in concert playing his guitar, and he seemed to be looking straight at me. His face looked ghostly white in the dim dawn light filtering through the half-open curtains, and his eyes, accusing, bore right through me. He knew what we had done; he had been watching. As I stared at the poster, I grew more and more uneasy. I felt as though Jimi could somehow tell Michael about what he had seen – that Michael would know just by looking into Jimi's burning eyes. I could almost hear his voice in my head: *Traitor.*

I had been lying awake thinking about what had happened, wondering if there was any way it could have been avoided. Now there was no turning back. Now that I had finally had Lisa, I needed to have her again, to hold her again. Not to do so would kill me, in spite of the ugliness I felt inside about betraying Michael. That feeling alone made me feel sick, especially after remembering all the happy times the three of us had spent together. The other feeling I had was that I would continue to see Lisa even though doing so would destroy the lives of all three of us. I felt empty, hollow inside, except for the burning greedy ball of flame in my heart that was eating its way into my soul.

Just after four o'clock, I couldn't bear lying awake with Jimi Hendrix staring at me any more, so I got dressed and left, leaving Lisa sleeping.

*

I got on with the usual routines of my life over the next few days, trying not to think about Lisa, about what we had done, about Michael. Then on Wednesday Lisa showed up on my doorstep.

"I woke and you were gone," she said, before she'd even stepped over the threshold. "You haven't even called."

I ushered her inside quickly; terrified that someone would overhear. "You shouldn't be here," I said, thinking how ridiculous it was even as the words came out. There was no reason for her not to be there; she was always over at my place. I was panicking, and it frightened me. "Where's Michael?"

"He went to see a friend tonight."

"Does he know you're here?"

"Well, yes. He doesn't think anything of me coming to see you when he's away, you know that. He thinks it's strange we haven't seen anything of you for a while. Why haven't you called?"

"How could I call, after what happened? I've been trying to forget all about it."

"But it did happen, Todd." She hesitated, gazing at me. "Are you sorry it happened? Because I'm not."

"Of course I'm not sorry. It felt right. Everything about it felt right. But that doesn't stop me feeling like such a shit now."

She collapsed into a chair, covering her face with her hands. "What are we going to do? I love Michael more than anything. I never wanted to hurt him."

I could tell from the way she was shaking that she was crying. I offered her a crumpled tissue, feeling helpless and at a loss for words. I wasn't sure there was anything we could do. I knew by then that everything that was happening to us was completely beyond our control.

Somehow we ended up making love again that night, and I knew that the nightmare was just beginning. I will never forget the haunted look in Lisa's eyes as she left me to go home to Michael.

*

I could not avoid Michael and Lisa indefinitely. I was so much a part of their lives that my absence would be noticeable. Michael phoned me up a week after the night Lisa came to visit.

"Todd, how are you? We haven't seen you for a while."

"Well, you know how things are," I said, trying to sound cheerful. The words made me cringe as soon as they were out of my mouth; it sounded such a stupid thing to say.

"Well, will you be round tomorrow?"

"I don't know." My Thursday nights had habitually been spent round at Michael and Lisa's place. Michael knew my life so well that I couldn't think of any excuse that would sound feasible enough.

"I've got a new Stones song book," Michael said. "If you bring your bass round, we can work through it."

Not being able to think of a reason to refuse, I found myself agreeing with a sinking heart.

I turned up the next evening, with my bass as Michael had requested, though I didn't know if I had it in my heart to play. I wasn't sure if I'd ever be able to play again. Lisa let me in. She looked haggard, as if it had been a long time since she'd had a decent night's sleep.

Michael sat on the sofa, playing 'Let's Spend the Night Together' on his guitar. Lisa and I exchanged glances. She mumbled something about making tea and disappeared into the kitchen. I greeted Michael with a smile pasted on my face, put the bass on the floor, and began to open the case. My hands shook as I fumbled with the clasps.

Michael was asking me cheerful questions about work, my parents, and the usual small talk. I rattled off the obligatory answers, telling myself fiercely to calm down, loosen up, try to be normal.

I didn't think I'd ever be normal again. "I've not been doing much playing for a while, Mike," I said. "I don't know if I can get into the right mood for the Stones."

Michael shrugged. "I only bought this book at the weekend so I've been playing around with it all week. But we don't have to play." He strummed a few experimental riffs. Lisa came back into the room with three mugs of tea, looking from me to Michael and back again. I wondered if she was comparing us. Physically Michael and I were very different. He was big and blond with a powerful build; I was smaller, slighter, and dark-haired. If I ever had to fight him, I didn't doubt he would beat me to a pulp. But I also knew that brute strength wasn't his style; he was far too intelligent. I found myself wondering what he would do if he knew what had been going on between Lisa and me.

I realised with a start that Michael had lapsed into 'Hey Joe'. It was one of his favourite Hendrix songs, but it sounded slicker than last time I heard him play it.

"You've been working on the Hendrix, Mike," I said.

"They don't come any better than Hendrix," Michael said. "I can't really do him justice. But I've been practising. Hendrix inspires me. You know that poster in the bedroom?"

My words caught in my throat, remembering how Jimi's eyes had borne down on me that first night with Lisa. I saw Lisa sitting on the floor across the room, staring at me anxiously.

Michael continued without waiting for an answer. "I go in there to play quite a lot. Jimi gives me inspiration. Sometimes I talk to him and, you know, I really believe he listens."

"I keep telling you to move that poster out of there," Lisa said. "It gives me the creeps. Those eyes ... I feel like they're watching me when I'm sleeping." She shuddered. "I can't stand Jimi Hendrix."

Michael smiled. "Can you believe it, Todd? I end up with a girlfriend who hates Hendrix." He looked at Lisa. "You know you have nothing to fear while Hendrix is looking after you."

He went back to strumming softly. The words of the song – about a man shooting his unfaithful woman who'd been messing around with another man – resounded through my guilt-ridden conscience over and over again.

In spite of feeling ripped apart by the guilt, Lisa and I continued to find places to meet, times to see each other. It was like an addiction. Each time we parted the great black void that was consuming me inside got a bit bigger, but still I could not stop thinking about Lisa, and when I could see her again.

I had to keep up the pretence of going to see her and Michael. He never acted like anything was wrong, like he suspected anything. He must have found out somehow. Maybe he guessed – he knew both of us so well. Maybe he was right about Jimi listening.

Things had been going on this way for about a month when Michael called me. "I have to go to see a customer in Glasgow next Monday," he said. "I'll be away overnight. Can you stay with Lisa for the night?"

"Ah ... I guess so," I stammered. My first thought was that he suspected and was testing me. "You want me to sleep on the sofa?"

"Well, I didn't think you'd want to sleep on the floor," Michael replied irritably.

"No, no, of course not."

"Thanks. I worry about Lisa being alone when I'm away. I know she'll be all right if you're with her."

The notion of Michael having such trust in me to leave me alone with his girlfriend, under the circumstances, might have been funny had the heaviness of my guilty conscience not destroyed my sense of humour. The same guilt was probably also responsible for me suddenly acquiring a suspicious nature. Something about the set-up seemed wrong to me. I phoned Lisa at work the following day.

"Was it your idea to have me stay over next week when Michael's away?" I asked.

"Of course not," Lisa snapped. "Do you think I could have the nerve to suggest something like that, given the state I'm in? It was his idea. He said he'd be happier leaving me if I had company."

"That's what he said to me, but I still don't like it. Do you think he suspects anything?"

"Why would he want to leave us alone together if he did? I have to go now. I'll see you next week."

I found myself saying goodbye to a dead line.

*

"I can sleep out here if you want me to, you know," I said. Lisa and I had been sitting stiffly side by side pretending to watch television for over an hour. Neither of us had spoken a word to each other in that time. A neat pile of pillows and blankets rested on the arm of the sofa.

"You know as well as I do that bedding won't get used tonight."

"What do you want from me, Lisa? Where's it going to end?"

"I'd give anything to be able to answer that," she replied flatly. "We can't go on seeing each other, but we can't stop seeing each other. Neither of us wants to hurt Michael, but we do it anyway. We don't have control anymore about where it all ends." She got up abruptly. "I'm going to bed."

I continued watching the film on TV, but I wasn't concentrating on it. My head was going round and round. Lisa was right; we had no control over this. I didn't believe we'd ever had any control over it. I knew that tonight I would once again end up in Lisa's bed, and this time it was Michael who'd brought us together. I turned off the TV and headed into the bathroom.

While I was brushing my teeth I noticed two toothbrushes in the holder beneath the bathroom cabinet. Michael had forgotten his toothbrush. I didn't think much of it at the time. People do forget things when they spend a night away.

I had that damned poster staring at me again as I fell asleep, and I dreamed about Jimi Hendrix. He was in concert, working himself into a glazed-eyed frenzy as he played the sort of wild guitar solo he was famous for. At the end of the solo he threw his guitar down onto the stage and set fire to it. The crowd screamed in ecstasy. Jimi was kneeling by the guitar, fanning it to make sure the flames took hold. Then he had a can of lighter fluid in his hand, squirting it over the guitar to give fuel to the blaze. A wall of flame shot up from the stage, thick black smoke curling out into the audience. I could feel the smoke in my throat, smell the acrid odour of burning wood and paint.

I sat up in bed. I tried to shake the grogginess of sleep from my head; my addled brain was beginning to register that the smoke was not part of the dream. It hung in the room.

I floundered to throw off the covers, and shook Lisa violently. "Wake up! Wake up! Lisa! There's a fire!"

"What?" she mumbled. She rolled over, stared at me, puzzled.

"There's a fire." Hastily I pulled my jeans on. The room was filling with smoke: I could see it coming in from under the door in thick clouds.

I yanked open the curtain, peering out of the window. It was pitch black outside. We were on the fifth floor – very high to jump, but there was grass on the ground. I struggled to open the window; it was jammed. I banged the frame desperately.

On the road beyond a figure moved. I became aware of two things simultaneously: one was that the white-faced figure on the road was Michael, staring blankly up at me, and the other was that the odour in the air I had thought was lighter fluid in my dream was actually petrol. Then everything happened at once.

I saw Lisa at the bedroom door. I started to scream at her not to open it, but it was too late. Flames engulfed the room. I could hear screams everywhere; I don't know if they were mine or Lisa's. The window I had been pounding on shattered and my bare arm was hanging out of it, wet with blood. I could feel the flames licking the bare flesh of my back and an excruciating pain ripping through my body. I started falling. Glass flew everywhere.

I remember very little after that. I spent a long time in hospital. It seems that Lisa died in the fire. I never did find out what happened to Michael. I don't think there was enough evidence in the end to pin the fire on him, but I knew it had been him who started it. In setting fire to his own flat, not only did he kill Lisa, he also destroyed his beloved record collection.

The knowledge of what Lisa and I had been doing must have destroyed him more than we had ever imagined. We both lost Lisa. I broke my spine and lost the use of my legs, and even after all the plastic surgery I still avoid looking into mirrors. My bitterest regret is that we didn't all die that night.

I still wonder how Michael found out about me and Lisa. Perhaps Jimi Hendrix told him after all.

# Trio

"A brother," Alison said confidently. I saw her looking at me with a half-smile on her face, pleased with the answer. "Yes. I see you as a brother." She was answering a question I had asked her over ten minutes ago.

It was the answer I had been more or less expecting. We walked side by side through the dry leaves littering the pavement. It was getting on for winter, I thought fleetingly as I stuffed my chilled hands deeper into the pockets of my fleece-lined jacket. Above us the bare branches swayed as the wind blew starkly about our ears.

"David?" Alison said.

"Mmm," I responded absently. I glanced at her, and saw she was studying me curiously. She was shorter than me, and I found myself wondering when that had happened. She was eighteen months older than me, and at first she had been taller. Then, for a long time we had been the same height. Now, suddenly, I was a couple of inches taller.

"What do you suppose would have happened if our relationship had developed into something else? Something ... more than friendship?"

I looked at her for a moment, trying to visualise her as someone else. I watched her long brown hair blowing about untidily, and the buffeted ends of her ridiculously long scarf. The complexion of her face possessed a pallor that emphasised the thin red scar on her cheek. She turned her head, sensing me watching her and smiled again, a Mona Lisa-type smirk that was neither a grin nor a frown, and showed none of her teeth, which I knew to be slightly crooked. Her face, straight on, was not unattractive, but was too flawed to be beautiful. The scar was a little too noticeable, the nose slightly too large. On some days, though, she could look pretty – when she spent time doing her hair, applying make-up, putting on a nice dress. Even so, I could not imagine her as a lover. I could not remember much about the day we first met, but it was back in the days when football in the park was more interesting to me than girls. Over the years our friendship had grown, but if I had ever loved her as more than a friend, it had been as a sister. Yes, the mere thought of Alison being anything else seemed incestuous.

I realised with a start that she was still waiting for my answer. "I don't know," I said finally. "I just can't imagine it."

"No," she replied. "But I think things would have been different."

A single red VW Golf went by and rounded the corner up ahead, before the noise of the engine faded away, and we were alone again in silence except for the rustle of the wind in the leaves.

"In what way?" I asked. We had reached the intersection of Birch Avenue, and we crossed over automatically, with barely a glance for traffic. There were never any cars coming around that corner.

Alison shrugged, and tossed her head to get her hair out of her face. It was a gesture I had seen a hundred times before. Alison's hair had always been shaggy and rather untidy looking, no matter what she tried to do to it. "Circumstances would be changed. We might have gone to different places, known different people ..." She faltered.

"You're thinking of Sandy, aren't you?"

Alison did not reply. Her expression was blank, but I saw a flicker of emotion in her eyes. I had come to know Alison's eyes. They were a pale, pure green, set far apart, and though Alison herself rarely expressed her feelings, her eyes always gave them away.

"Do you remember the first words you ever said to me?" she said suddenly.

"It was at the audition for *Peter Pan*," I said uncertainly, for I did not remember.

"You kept looking at me, all the time we were sitting waiting to go up," Alison went on. "Then, when we were packing up to go, you came marching over to me and said, 'I know you from somewhere'." She smiled. "Not 'hello', or 'what's your name?' but 'I know you from somewhere'."

"And what did you say?"

"Don't you remember?"

"I remember I was trying to make conversation," I replied. "I was twelve years old, in a room full of strangers. I had never been to an audition before, and I was incredibly nervous. Yours seemed to be a friendly face, so I decided to try talking to you."

"You were only little, weren't you? I was thirteen, I think – yes, because you came to my fourteenth birthday party. Sandy must have been fourteen."

"I remember that party. We went to the park, about ten o'clock. Everyone else ran off and left us there, you and me and Sandy."

"Then when they came back, we hid from them." Alison turned to me, and I saw my miniaturised image in duplicate, reflected in the green of her eyes. "That was the way it was from then on. The three of us against the world."

"They started calling us the Terrible Trio at the Little Theatre, didn't they? God, that was ten years ago. Practically another lifetime."

"It was another lifetime." Alison shoved her hands into her pockets and fell silent, watching her feet as they scattered the dead leaves through the mud. We had passed the end of the cul-de-sac, and were walking through the clearing in the woods, a dirt path made slimy by the autumn rain and the passage of many rubber boots. I was wearing trainers, having forgotten that we would be going through the woods. I tried to step carefully, watching that the mud did not ooze its way under the tongues. I did not relish the thought of scrubbing off my shoes later on. Alison was wearing winter boots and a thick coat, not surprisingly. She started dressing for winter in September and stayed that way until March. I had never known anyone to complain of being cold as much as Alison did.

"The night of the accident," she said suddenly. "If it had been a date, just you and me ... Sandy wouldn't have been with us."

"But you can't say that. Who's to say what would have happened if things had been different? We can't change the past." We emerged from the woods at the back of the cemetery. As we followed the iron railings around, I was struck once more by the atmosphere that hung over the gravestones. Such an air of silence and stillness, so much so that I always felt compelled to whisper and creep about when I went amongst the graves. As if afraid of disturbing the dead.

"Sandy was driving, don't forget," I reminded Alison. I watched her hand go almost unconsciously to the scar on her cheek, her only visible reminder of the crash. I had no such disfigurement, no lasting injuries to have to come to terms with. I had been in the back seat and very, very lucky.

Alison was silent, and I was acutely aware of the distance between us, not physically, but mentally. "Do you realise," I said, "that this is the first time we've been out together since the accident?"

"Yes, I know," Alison said quietly. We reached the wrought iron gates, and entered the cemetery together. The gravestones stood in rows like stone soldiers, and it seemed to me the ghostly eyes of all those buried there were watching us pass by.

Alison did not speak again until we reached Sandy's grave. It was right at the back of the cemetery with the other more recent tombs, a sad, bare patch of earth marked with a small marble headstone, simply shaped and simply worded:

SANDRA LOUISE FLETCHER

1986 – 2008

SADLY MISSED

We stood on either side, looking solemnly down at the words etched into the marble. "We should have brought flowers," Alison said. "It looks so sad."

"Sandy wouldn't have wanted flowers," I answered. "She didn't like wasting money on things that would wither and die so quickly. She relished life."

"And now it's been taken from her." Alison looked levelly at me. "She took life away from all of us."

"What do you mean?" I asked. But I knew. And Alison, gazing at me with blank green eyes, realised that. Alison, Sandy and I had been a team. One for all and all for one, since childhood, with Sandy being forever the heart and soul of the group. Now that she was gone, the life was gone, the team had disintegrated.

"It could have been different, David," Alison said sadly. "Instead we settled for a three-way friendship."

"But I never loved you that way."

"I loved you," she replied, and for a minute I thought I saw something in her eyes, as though that quiet statement had been a revelation to her, but it passed so quickly I wasn't sure if it had ever been there at all.

"We were just kids when we became friends. But that friendship has been something very special. We've grown up together."

"It was special." Alison shook her head. "No more. Two years, David, since Sandy died. Our friendship revolved around three; with two it can't exist. Have we talked since the accident? I mean *really* talked, the way we used to before, with Sandy? We don't have anything to say to each other. It's over."

I stood still, numb, unable to believe what I was hearing. "We've been friends for ten years, Alison. Doesn't that mean anything to you?"

"Yes. It does. That's why I have to go." She turned away, looking down at her foot as it stirred the grass at the graveside. "I'm going away next week."

"Away?" I repeated stupidly. "Where?"

She shrugged. "Canada, maybe. I've got relatives there. I don't really know where I'm going. I've got some savings put by."

"Will I ever see you again?" I asked. I saw the answer I feared in her eyes, but she turned away from me without a word.

"Goodbye, David," she said finally. I remained frozen to the spot as she walked away from me, wanting to go after her but for some reason unable to. She did not look back, and I watched her retreating figure until I could see it no more. Her walk was slow and heavy, black-stockinged legs visible only from the knee down beneath the hem of her bulky blue coat. Her hands were in her pockets, the ends of her scarf trailing, and her hair falling carelessly down her back. It was getting very long now, I realised. She had been trying to grow it for years.

She walked back the way she had come, and when she went through the cemetery gates I lost sight of her. I turned back to the headstone feeling suddenly, desolately alone.

I stood and hunched over the grave for a long time before I finally started to make my way home.

Two days later, I heard about Alison's death on the radio. She had driven her car off the road. I will never know whether it was an accident, or deliberate. But it is a strange coincidence that my two closest friends both met their deaths in car accidents within two years of each other. Once a month I take a Sunday afternoon and visit both graves. Perhaps I am being silly but I don't drive anywhere anymore. I can't help wondering if the trio was doomed from the start.

I cannot differentiate the seasons anymore; it always seems cold to me. I feel perpetually on the brink of winter. Life goes on, even when lonely. I have had a few successful, albeit short-lived, relationships, and even more unsuccessful ones, but I am still alone. No one else will ever know me as well as Alison and Sandy did.

It's just so cold ...

# To Dream of An Angel

The discussion that night steered away from the story we were meant to be workshopping, as it often did. We ended up talking about dreams. I seem to recall that the conversation centred around the argument that dreams are but a distortion of reality.

It was John's story that started it off, a floating, surreal piece of writing that continuously flitted between fantasy and reality. How we progressed from there I can't really remember. Someone said that dreams are fragments of a past reality – half-remembered details from a former incarnation. Someone else suggested they were remnants of a daily reality – the mind, in effect, has a clear-out while we sleep, storing away the day's thoughts and experiences in a logical order and casting out those it does not wish to keep.

Dean did not put forth his opinion, as I recall. Instead, he said something like "it's going to be a long night" and went to make more coffee. It was his flat the five of us invaded once a fortnight, to critique each other's writing. At least that was the intention. Most of the time we got side-tracked into discussing something totally unrelated to the story at hand.

As for myself, I have always believed that dreams are messages from the subconscious mind. Each one has a hidden meaning that must be interpreted in order to benefit from the message. But in looking for the meanings in dreams, perhaps we overlook the real message. When does a dream become a reality – or, in fact, does a dream ever stop being a reality? I had a graphically passionate dream once involving my friend Simon – a dream whose intensity rattled me so much I decided at the time not to mention it to either my boyfriend or Simon. Three months later, Simon and I were living together. Was the dream a glimpse of the reality to come, or was it an indication of my subconscious desire, a desire that eventually surfaced and caused the dream to become reality?

I have had many dreams in which I am kissing a man with whom I have never had any romantic connections, or even secret desires. These dreams never were, nor ever will be, reality. So what's the meaning there?

I went home thinking about our conversation, and that night I had a dream. I was standing in a cobbled street, like the ones portrayed in Elizabethan times. It was market day, and the sights and sounds of barter went on all around me. Suddenly the sky became dark, and the people were thrown into a panic. I was filled with dread. I looked up as all the citizens hastily gathered their wares and scurried to the sanctuary of the surrounding buildings. A great dark shape loomed in the sky, a shadowy head with an indefinable body, and I knew instinctively that this was a demon.

I stood in the street and saw that in my outstretched hand I held a knife with a polished wooden handle. It felt very heavy, and it got increasingly heavier as I continued to hold it. I looked up and saw Dean standing before me. He was dressed in black. "I am the demon," he said.

I held the knife out to him. "Take it. It's too heavy."

"Too heavy for a knife?"

"It's heavier than I thought it would be. Why is it so heavy?"

"If it gets too heavy, drop it," Dean said.

I let the knife fall.

Then I was standing in a green meadow, with a yellow sun shining down from a bright blue sky. I felt at peace. In my left hand I clutched a talisman that I recognised, a five-pointed star with a gem set in the centre, that somehow I was not surprised to see. I heard someone calling my name – "Jenny! Jenny!"

I turned around to see Simon running through the fields towards me. He was smiling radiantly, and to me he looked just like an angel. I rushed to meet him, and I tied the talisman on its leather strap around his neck. He lifted me up and swung me round. I felt an absurd sensation of indescribable joy, as if the happiness of thousands of people channelled through me.

And I woke up. The radio alarm clock was relaying the seven o'clock news, and through half-open curtains the first dim light of dawn filtered through. Beside me, Simon rolled over with a groan, reaching out an arm to stab at the radio buttons. He opened his eyes, bleary with sleep, and blinked at me. I propped myself up on an arm and smiled down at him.

"Whassup?" he mumbled, flopping back onto the pillow.

"You look like an angel," I told him. I gave him a kiss.

I relayed my dream to him over breakfast. "You saw Dean last night," he said. "That's why you dreamed about him."

"I saw the rest of my writing group last night as well. None of them were in the dream."

Simon rolled his eyes at me over his newspaper. "Maybe they'll be in tonight's episode."

I sighed. "Finish your cereal."

*

Work that day was particularly exhausting, and walking to the station I thought of nothing but going home and relaxing in a steaming bath. But instead of taking the train home to Croydon, I found myself on my way to Beckenham. I had a sudden compulsion to talk to Dean. When I showed up on his doorstep, he didn't seem surprised to see me.

"All that talk about dreams last night must have got my imagination going," I said.

He regarded me thoughtfully. "You had a dream last night," he said. It was a statement, not a question. "You dreamed about demons, and meadows, and knives. And me."

"How did you know?"

Dean scratched his chin. "Intuition," he said after a moment. "Like I knew you'd be round here tonight. Hold on a sec." He got up and left the room.

I shuffled around on the battered sofa, trying to relax. I couldn't understand the reason for my apprehension. There were still blankets on the sofa from a couple of weeks ago, when I'd complained of feeling cold at a meeting. Dean's living room was never tidy, but since most of the clutter consisted of books, it had always seemed friendly to me. One wall was completely covered with bookshelves made up of bricks and long planks of wood. Most of the books were horror and science fiction paperbacks; there must have been over two hundred in all. Near the top was a row of books on magic spells and rituals. Dean was what I would phrase as a white witch.

He came back into the room with a long candle.

"Remember that night a few weeks ago, when I came over and we talked about magic?" I asked him. I had been doing some research for a story I was working on at the time. "You got me to hold the knife and then the talisman, and tell you what I saw? I saw the same images in my dream last night, but in reverse. I held the knife and saw the market, and the demon, and the field when I had the talisman. In reality it was the other way around."

"There's that word again. Reality." Dean cleared a space on his cluttered coffee table for the candle, and lit it. "What is reality? What are dreams?"

"We argued that all last night, and reached no conclusions."

"I'm not saying we'll come to any conclusions. I want to try a little experiment."

"What sort of experiment?"

"A bit like the knife and the talisman," Dean said. "Look at the candle."

I obeyed. Out of the corner of my eye I saw Dean get up to turn out the lights. He returned and stood on the other side of the candle.

"Shall I stand up?" I asked. "No, you're fine sat there. Just relax. Concentrate on the flame."

He crouched down, eye-level to the flame, his face, reflecting orange in the dancing light, and his long hair highlighted a few shades lighter, almost copper-coloured. The gem in the talisman around his neck seemed to shimmer, and I noticed he was wearing black. He was staring at me intently.

"Close your eyes," Dean said softly. His voice was soothing, the flame mesmerising. I closed my heavy eyelids, feeling myself drifting into sleep.

Suddenly I was on the ceiling, looking down at the darkened room. I saw the candle burning steadily. I saw myself, motionless, lying stretched out amongst the blankets. I looked as if I'd fallen over sideways, with one arm pinned beneath my body. I saw Dean hurry over, bending over me.

Then I was being swooped away, wind rushing past my ears, through the roof of the building and off into space.

I came down in a field, landing very gently on the soles of my bare feet. A warm breeze caressed my face, the light from the sun so bright it hurt my eyes, and I could almost imagine airily romantic music playing, like in a corny film.

I recognised the field, of course. Simon was there, smiling at me, his hair almost glowing, creating a blonde halo around his head. "I'm glad you're here," he said.

"I'm not meant to be here. I have to go back."

"Please don't go, Jenny. I'm so afraid."

I wanted to reach out to him, to hold him, but I was snatched away, as if I was being sucked into a whirlpool, air and water whipping against my body.

I sat up with a jolt on Dean's sofa. Dean grabbed me as I fell forward, his expression a confused mix of fear and relief. "Jesus, Jenny, you scared me. You stopped breathing. Are you alright?"

"I died," I said.

"You projected, didn't you?"

"I died," I repeated.

"What happened? What did you see?" Dean went to switch the light on.

"It was the field again. Simon was there. But if I died, then he must have as well. Simon's dead." The realisation hit me suddenly, with astounding clarity. Yet I felt nothing but a profound emptiness.

Dean blew out the candle. "I'm sorry. That got out of hand."

"It's true," I murmured. "Dreams are reality. Nobody can know where they stop, and reality begins. I have to go home."

"Are you sure you're okay? You should stay here a while and rest. Get your bearings back."

"No, I'm fine. Really."

Dean was very reluctant to let me go, but I bade him farewell. I checked the news on my phone on the way home, but there was nothing. It would be too soon for it to be in the news. I thought about Simon as I stared out of the grimy train window. What had he been wearing when he left for work that morning? I pictured him in my mind. Blue suit, blue tie, white shirt. I had bought him that tie. Blonde, collar length hair, blue eyes ...

My face was wet with tears by the time I got home. I switched on the TV before I had even taken off my coat, and kept it on the BBC news channel all evening. There was nothing.

Simon should have been home by six. Sometimes he worked late. If he was home late, it was no big deal. But not today. Today he left work on time. I knew. I couldn't explain my feelings. I had fallen asleep at Dean's place and had a strange dream, that's all. There was no logic to my apprehension. But still, somehow, I knew instinctively that Simon was not coming home.

I prowled around the silent, empty house, my mind spinning. At seven o'clock I put my mobile phone on the coffee table and sat on the sofa, staring at it. From the hallway the clock kept on ticking, sounding ominously loud. I just sat there staring at the phone, waiting for it to ring. Waiting for the call that I knew was going to come.

# Kay's Blues

Pain thudded behind Kay's eyes. She passed her twenty-pound note to the white-coated young man behind the pharmacy counter, and waited as he put her purchases into a plastic bag: a box of Tampax, a pack of Stayfrees, and a big bottle of Nurofen.

"Kay! I thought that was you," said a bright voice behind her. Kay turned around, a fresh stab of pain slicing its way through her head.

"Hi, Caroline," Kay said wearily to the short blonde girl who had appeared beside her.

"I've been following you from the tube station. I called out, but you didn't hear me."

"Sorry," Kay mumbled. "I'm a bit out of it today." She took the plastic bag from the pharmacist, who wore a straight-from-the packet smile on his face as he handed Kay her change.

"It's alright for him to smile," Kay muttered savagely as she stormed out of Boots. "What does he know about how I'm feeling? What do men know about pain?"

"That time of the month?" Caroline asked, hurrying to keep up with her taller friend.

Kay stopped outside the door and fumbled inside the plastic bag for the Nurofen container. "If men had to put up with period pains, they would have been eradicated years ago."

"I know," said Caroline sympathetically. "It's an effort to even get out of bed when you feel like you've got a dwarf swinging from your kidneys."

Kay shook a couple of pills from the bottle and swallowed them dry before stuffing the bottle back into the bag. "That," she said to her friend, "is a pretty accurate summing up of period pain. Not forgetting, of course, the headache, the depression, and the general sensation of feeling like shit."

"If it's that bad, why don't you go home? I'll tell Alan you're not well."

"It's no worse than last month, or the month before that, and it'll probably be just the same next month. I can't take a week out of every month off sick and still expect to have a job. What gets me most," Kay went on angrily, "is that this time it's started sooner than it should have done. Either I'm going to be early or there'll be an extra two days of agony. And I'm never early."

They came to a stop outside the Charing Cross Road book shop in which they both worked. Kay glared at the building, feeling a hatred for it and what it represented that extended to the very bricks themselves. "God, I don't know how I'm going to face customers today. I'm really not in the mood."

Caroline linked her arm through Kay's. "I'll speak to Alan. Perhaps he'll put us in the stock room and then you won't have to speak to anyone. Come on, it's time for work."

*

Caroline's appeal to the shop manager was successful, and Kay managed to hide in the stock room for most of the day, under the guise of counting Arrow paperbacks.

"You seeing Dylan tonight?" Caroline asked. She was unpacking the Transworld order that had arrived late yesterday.

"He called last night," Kay replied. "But I hope he doesn't come round. I'm in no mood for company."

A dark-haired, male head appeared from behind a pile of boxes. "What sort of a name is Dylan, anyway?"

"A very good one for a guitarist," Kay said. "Who rattled your cage, anyway, Rob?"

A pair of shoulders followed the head out from behind the boxes. "If you have your conversations within my earshot, they're not private. Wasn't Dylan the stoned-out rabbit in 'The Magic Roundabout'?"

"He was a guitarist as well," Kay replied. "As it happens, I understand my Dylan was named after Dylan Thomas."

"Why?" asked Rob.

"How the hell should I know?" Kay said, irritated. "I guess his parents are into poetry."

"How long have you been seeing this guy? A couple of weeks?"

"More like a month, actually. Not that it's any of your business."

"Well, what happened to James? I remember you talking about James. And before that there was Kevin."

"Rob!" Caroline said sternly. "Didn't your mother ever teach you it's rude to ask personal questions?"

Rob shrugged. "I remember Kevin. He came to that pub night we had in the summer. I spent quite a long time talking to him."

"Kevin was an idiot," Caroline said.

"I thought he was alright," said Rob. "A bit boring, maybe. Spent all night going on about his car. Who gives a toss about his fuel-injected engine, I say?"

"And I say you should mind your own fucking business," Kay snapped. She threw her clipboard at Rob and stormed out of the stock room.

Caroline glared at Rob, who had been too surprised to duck. He stood rubbing his shoulder, where the clipboard had caught him before it clattered to the floor. "Look what you've done now," she said.

"What did I say?" Rob looked bewildered. "What's wrong with her today?"

"I don't expect you to understand." Caroline stepped past Rob and went in search of Kay.

She found her friend in the staff kitchen. "Don't let him get to you, Kay, he's just –" She stopped. Kay was hanging her head over the sink, pills clutched in her fist. "Kay, what are you doing?"

"Trying to stop the pain," Kay mumbled dully.

"You mustn't take that many." Caroline prised the pills from Kay's hand.

"I'm just tired of it, Caz," Kay wailed. "Every bloody month my life is hell for a week. I can't stand it any more."

"Why don't you go back to the doctor?" Caroline led Kay away from the sink and lowered her gently into a chair.

"I'm sick of going to the doctor. The doctors have run out of suggestions. I've tried everything. Nothing works." She dissolved into tears, sobbing into Caroline's shoulder.

Caroline patted her friend on the back awkwardly. "Go home to bed," she said. "I'll tell Alan you've gone home sick."

\*

Sunday came. Kay hated Sundays. The headache had stayed away for a couple of days, but her mood had not improved. She lolled about all day. She didn't feel up to going anywhere or seeing anyone, so she stayed in and got more depressed because she was alone. Feeling bored but not wanting to do anything. Feeling lonely but not wanting to see anyone. There was never a reason for feeling irritable and depressed during the week or so she had come to know as her 'Blues', but it always happened, and now she expected it. She got through it by remembering that one morning she would wake up and it would have disappeared. Nothing would have changed; her life had never drastically improved overnight – but the depression had gone away.

She had not heard from Dylan since he'd phoned her four days ago, and that suited her fine. Not that she didn't want to see him; she just knew that she would take out her hostility on him, as she had with other men who had passed through her life. Men never understood how she felt when she was like this. The only thing she could do was avoid them until it was all over.

She lay sprawled on the sofa. The TV was on, but she couldn't concentrate. She was thinking about Kevin. He'd been a creep, undoubtedly, but maybe he hadn't deserved it. Just because he happened to have called on her during the week she was suffering from her Blues, had she really been justified in treating him the way she did? She had not seen Kevin since that day.

At six o'clock the doorbell rang, disturbing Kay from the misery she had immersed herself in. She grumbled to herself and rolled off the sofa, shuffling to the door in her socks.

Dylan stood on the other side of the door, grinning broadly. He was carrying a bunch of daffodils. Kay's first reaction was irritation. Here she stood in her old track suit bottoms and a scruffy T-shirt, with hair that needed washing, and there was Dylan looking for an evening of romance.

"I can't help feeling you've been avoiding me," he said.

"What are you doing here?" Kay scowled.

"I've come to look after you. Can I come in?"

Kay sighed, and stepped back from the door to admit him. "Since you're here, you may as well."

"You don't sound very pleased to see me. Are you still feeling ill?"

"I'm feeling just swell," Kay said sarcastically, thinking about how terrible she must have looked.

"What is it?" Dylan persisted, concern in his voice. "Is it some sort of bug? Have you been to a doctor?"

"No, it's not a bug. It's just … " Kay hesitated. "It's just that time of the month, that's all."

"Why didn't you tell me? Did you think I wouldn't understand?"

"Most men don't."

"Poor baby." Dylan took Kay's hand and led her back into the living room. "Why don't you lie down, and I'll fix dinner." He settled her on the sofa.

Kay continued to lay there as Dylan fussed about, getting her blanket, putting the flowers in water and arranging them on the table, making her a cup of tea. She knew he was trying to be helpful, but all she wanted was to be left alone in her misery. Couldn't he see that?

She heard him clattering about in the kitchen, getting together pots and pans. Every sound grated on her nerves. Eventually he poked his head around the door.

"Where do you keep the cooking oil?"

"In the cupboard," Kay sighed, without looking up.

Dylan's head retreated back into the kitchen. "The one above the sink?" he called out a moment later.

"No, the other one," Kay shouted back irritably. "No – wait a minute." She hauled herself to her feet, tossing back the blanket Dylan had carefully tucked round her, and shuffled into the kitchen.

Dylan was hunting about in the cupboards. A sauce of something simmered on the stove. He'd been chopping vegetables; a little pile of mushrooms and peppers littered the counter. "What have you been doing in here?" Kay demanded.

Dylan grinned. "It'll be good. Trust me. But I can't find the cooking oil."

Kay opened another cupboard above her head, pulled out a bottle of vegetable oil and thrust it at him. Dylan still had his head in the other cupboards. "Now what are you looking for?"

"Frying pan," Dylan said.

"Oh for heaven's sake." Kay yanked open the door of the cupboard under the sink, and pulled out the frying pan.

"Now go and lie down and let me take care of everything," Dylan said.

"What, and ruin my kitchen? I might be better off doing it myself. Look at the mess you've made."

"I do tidy up after myself. In fact, I was even planning on doing your dishes for you as well." Dylan gestured at the sink, which was piled high with dirty pots, some of which were a good three days old.

"Oh, I see, you're insinuating that I'm a slob now, are you?"

"I'm insinuating no such thing. Why are you so touchy?"

"I'm not touchy," Kay shouted. "I didn't ask you to come round and bother me."

Dylan looked crushed. "I thought you might appreciate a bit of company. I can always go if you want me to."

"Don't you dare go and leave this mess for me to clean up." Kay picked up the chopping knife, lying on the counter with the vegetables, and waved it at him aggressively.

Dylan looked at her for a moment. "Look, I know you're not well. So why don't you go back into the other room, and let me finish making dinner." He took Kay's arm.

She shook him off savagely. "Don't touch me. I can walk."

"Okay." Dylan took a step backwards, hands outstretched.

Kay sat down on the sofa, absently cradling the knife handle in her hands, wallowing in her depression. She was twenty-eight years old and still a shop assistant. What happened to all the grand plans she had made with her friends at school? She had no career prospects, no husband, no kids, and could not think of a single thing in her future to look forward to.

"You know we ought to talk about what we're going to get John and Debbie as a wedding present," Dylan called out from the kitchen.

"Who?"

Dylan appeared round the door. "My brother. He gets married next month. I told you about it."

"I didn't realise I was expected to go to the wedding."

"Well, of course. Why not?"

"You and I have known each other all of three weeks and already you want to drag me to family functions?" Kay said irritably.

"I'd like you to go. I'd like you to meet my family."

"I don't want to meet your family. I hate family gatherings."

"Come on, Kay, don't be like that. I thought you and I had something going."

"Just because I've invited you into my bed doesn't mean I am inviting you to run my life."

Dylan wore a hurt expression. "None of this has meant anything to you? I thought it was something special."

From the kitchen came sizzling noises and a great deal of smoke. Dylan leapt back into the kitchen, swearing under his breath. A moment later the smoke alarm began to shriek.

*Oh God, that's all I need,* Kay thought, holding her head with both hands. Her brain felt like it was going to explode. "Switch it off for God's sake," she screamed. She leapt to her feet.

Dylan collided with her as he came running out of the kitchen. He grabbed one of the chairs from around the dining table and hurried out into the corridor. One of the chair legs caught Kay's shin as he passed by.

"Be careful, you idiot," she screamed at him. From the kitchen, smoke still billowed from the sizzling mass of vegetables on the stove.

"Sorry," Dylan muttered. He was standing on the chair beneath the smoke alarm, blowing on it in an attempt to stop the noise. Kay's leg hurt where the chair had hit it. It would come up in a big bruise by morning.

The smoke alarm fell mercifully silent. "You clumsy bastard!" Kay screamed, leaping at Dylan as he was about to climb down from the chair. She made a grab for the chair and rocked it, tipping Dylan to the floor. He cried out in surprise.

Kay fell on him before he could get up, sitting on his chest, her legs straddling his torso. "What's got into you?" Dylan gasped.

"I'm a fool, that's what," Kay shrieked. "You barge into my life and try to take it over, and I'm sick of it. Leave me alone, do you hear? Leave me alone!"

She lashed out with the knife, striking again and again, her own rage making her oblivious to Dylan's cries of pain.

Eventually she realised Dylan was silent and she stopped, letting the knife clatter to the floor. She crawled away from the inert body, staring at it in horror. She looked at her hands, her T-shirt, spattered with blood, and at the blood that leaked from Dylan's chest and was forming a growing puddle on the hallway floor.

She collapsed onto the sofa and began to cry, huge wracking sobs that came as if they would never stop. She hadn't wanted it to happen to Dylan. Why hadn't he left her alone when she asked him to? Why didn't they ever understand why she needed to be left alone?

She could argue that Kevin might have deserved it. But Dylan hadn't. She'd really liked Dylan.

# The Wedding Hat

"You must get a hat," Frances said, staring critically at the blue dress Alex was holding up.

"Why?" Alex said.

"Because it's a wedding. Everyone wears hats at weddings."

"I don't think Grace is going to care whether or not I wear a hat."

"Of course she will. She's the bride. She wants everything to be perfect. Everyone else will have a hat, and you simply must have one. That dress will be acceptable with a nice hat. Why don't we go shopping on Saturday, you and me, and I'll pick one for you?"

"No, Mother, it's fine," Alex said hastily. "I'll get myself a hat."

"Are you sure that's such a good idea, dear? You know what an appalling sense of style you've got."

"Thanks very much, Mother."

"I'm just saying what's true, dear. You slop around in scruffy T-shirts and ripped jeans most of the time. And you're always complaining about how much you hate shopping. I don't know how I ended up with a daughter who cares so little about her appearance. You must take after your father." Frances sniffed in disapproval.

"Mother, I'll get a hat. I promise. Now let's drop the subject."

And so Alex found herself sacrificing a Thursday afternoon to tramp down the High Street, determined to find something to keep her mother off her back. She had never worn a hat, and had no clue where to begin. Most of the ones she had looked at so far she had hated. The white straw effect ones with big floppy brims made her look like an outcast from *Charlie's Angels*. The pastel pink and blue ones with the ridiculous bows were only ever worn by the mother of the bride. And the twenties-style things – well, she just didn't like them. And all of them were extraordinarily expensive. Why someone would spend three hundred pounds on a hat they would probably only wear once was beyond Alex's comprehension.

Her feet were starting to hurt, and she was ready to kill for a cup of tea, but she knew that if she didn't buy something her mother would pick out something for her. She was just thinking that she'd have to go back to Debenham's and go for one of the floppy-brimmed ones when she spied a small shop, tucked away between a newsagent's and a shoe shop, with hats displayed on Styrofoam heads in the window. 'Accessory Magic' was emblazoned above the window in red and black letters.

Alex stepped into the shop, blinking her eyes in the dim interior. After the brightness of the sun outside, it took a while for her eyes to adapt. Eventually she could make out the contents of the shop. Scarves and necklaces of coloured jewels hung on hooks along one wall of the small shop. Along another, pairs of gloves and ear-rings on cardboard backs were displayed. In the corner by the window stood a shop mannequin, dressed in a beaded Indian skirt and matching camisole, a magnificent black feather boa draped around its neck. A hat of black creped velvet, decorated with red lace tied in an outlandish bow at the side, perched on its head.

Alex moved towards the back of the shop, where a number of hats were laid out on display shelves. She cast a disinterested eye along the wares. Again, none of these hats grabbed her attention. Then her gaze alighted on a dusty-looking hat, lying forgotten at the back of the shelf. She carefully retrieved it from behind a big straw number with a large silk rose attached.

The hat in Alex's hands was plain black, made out of some felt-like material. It had a short rigid brim, and a band of blue satin, ending in two tails which hung down the back like a gondolier's hat.

There was a mirror on the shelf. Alex tilted it forward so she could see her face, and put the hat on her head.

As she gazed at her reflection in the mirror, an image suddenly sprang into her mind. Standing on the edge of a bridge, feeling the metal cutting into the soles of her feet, her hands clutching the side, flakes of paint rubbing off against her palms. Staring down into the black swirling water far below, down, down ...

"Can I help you?" An old woman had materialised beside Alex, rubbing her wizened hands together in anticipation. She was tiny, dressed in unrelieved grey, her white hair pulled tight into a bun.

"Oh, er ..." Startled, Alex pulled the hat from her head. "Can you tell me how much this is, please?"

The old woman looked at Alex intently, and then looked at the hat she still clasped in her hand. "You like that one, eh? You think it suits you?"

"Well, that depends on how much it is."

"How much do you think it's worth?"

Alex sighed. "Look, I'm not in the mood to bargain. Just tell me how much it is."

"How much do you want to pay?"

"You're asking the wrong girl. I don't know anything about hats. This is something I'm being forced to buy for my cousin's stupid wedding, and I'm probably never going to wear it again. I want to pay about twenty quid for it, but I imagine it'll be horribly overpriced, like all of them seem to be. So just tell me how much you want for it and we can get the whole thing over and done with."

"Twenty pounds is all I ask from you for this hat."

"Oh," said Alex, surprised. "Well, in that case, I'll take it."

The old woman shuffled to the counter and began to ring Alex's purchase into the cash register. Alex crossed to the counter and put the hat down on it while she fumbled in her bag for her purse. The transaction completed, the old woman put Alex's new hat into a plain brown paper bag with sturdy handles. Alex thanked her as she took the bag.

"Mind what you are thankful for," the old woman said. "Blessings are so often curses, but it's too late before we see it."

Alex hurried out of the shop, deciding that woman was clearly not all there. She had looked way past retirement. Maybe she was the owner's mother, or something, and he humoured her because she had nothing else to do to pass the time.

She thought about her own mother. At least she had escaped Mother's choice of hat, and she'd found a perfectly acceptable one for only twenty quid. Perhaps her luck was in, at last.

\*

"Alexandra, do hurry up. We don't want to be late." Frances stood in the doorway, drumming white-gloved fingers on the door frame impatiently. She wore a pink wool twin set with a pink hat that sported a mess of lace winding round the top and falling over her face.

Alex was very glad that she had managed to find her own hat. The blue dress looked okay, now she was wearing it, and she had added a string of pearls her grandmother had given her years ago. Luckily, the pair of thick blue bangles she always wore to cover up the scars on her wrists went with the dress, because they were the same shade of blue. The band on the hat was the same colour, too. She put it on in front of the hall mirror.

*Cold metal underneath her feet. Falling down, down, towards the black water* ...

"Come on, darling, we must go. Carl is waiting in the car."

Alex shook her head to clear the image that had inexplicably appeared in it. "Alright, I'm coming." She picked up her handbag and fumbled with her keys, her mother waiting impatiently as she locked the flat.

Another image flashed into her mind as Alex looked at her mother: Frances, old and haggard, slumped in a faded armchair, a bottle of gin in her lap. Her arm flopped over the side of the chair, the lit cigarette falling from her fingers, the carpet beginning to smoulder ...

Alex frowned, shaking her head again. She followed her mother to the black BMW by the kerb, where her mother's latest suitor, Carl, was waiting.

"Mum, you're not drinking again, are you? I thought the doctor told you to stop."

Frances waved her hand dismissively. "Oh, what does he know? The odd G and T never hurt anyone."

Alex listened to Carl and her mother keep up a stream of jovial and inane conversation while she tried not to gag on her mother's perfume – as usual, it was something very expensive and she was wearing far too much of it. She hoped the inevitable question of her love life would not arise.

No such luck. "So darling, have you got a boyfriend yet?"

Alex sighed. "No, Mother, I'm not seeing anyone right now."

"Well really dear, if you made more of an effort to look nice, more boys would ask you out. You look nice today, you do. That dress suits you. You could have put some make-up on, though. And you really should consider a new hairstyle; you walk around looking like you've got a haystack on your head."

"Thank you, Mother. I don't want a boyfriend."

"What nonsense. Of course you want a boyfriend. You're twenty-eight years old, Alex. You haven't got many child bearing years left, you know. You really need to get a move on."

"Now that Lisa's satisfied your need to be a grandmother, can't you leave me alone?" Alex said irritably.

"I'm only thinking of you, darling. I don't like to see you unhappy."

"Who says I'm unhappy?"

"I know you are, darling. You don't have any friends, you never go out anywhere. It's not healthy to be holed up in that poky little flat all the time, wallowing in misery."

"I'm not wallowing in misery."

Frances fixed her with a determined stare. "You can't fool your mother, Alexandra." She turned to Carl. "She was such a cheerful little thing when she was a child, you know. Then she hit adolescence. She was thirteen when she attempted suicide the first time. I kept hoping she'd grow out of it."

"Mother," Alex snapped. "Drop it, please."

"Well, here we are," Carl announced, in what was obviously a blatant attempt to change the subject. "There's the church, over there."

Alex stared at the forbidding, gothic-looking structure as Carl pulled into the car park. As she picked up her hat and handbag and climbed out of the car, she wondered how many other relatives she would have to explain the non-existence of boyfriends to before the day was out.

*

All day strange images popped into Alex's head whenever she looked at people. Watching her twenty-year-old cousin Grace get married to Tim the stock broker, she saw an older, overweight Grace sitting alone in a grubby flat, three young children pulling at her clothes. She looked at Tim and saw him in a seedy hotel room with an attractive dark-haired woman. The dark-haired woman was telling Tim that she was pregnant.

When Alex looked at Grace's five-year-old sister Charlotte, a little blonde cherub kitted out in a lacy pink bridesmaid's dress, she saw a teenaged Charlotte, thin and gaunt, shooting up heroin in a filthy public toilet.

After the service she found Frances talking to Grace's mother. "So good to see you, Alexandra, dear," Aunt June said, smiling broadly. "It's been too long." As she took Alex's hand to shake it, Alex heard June say, "She always looks such a mess, and we never see her with men. I'm sure she's a lesbian. It'll be because she's had no positive female role models."

Alex, startled, stared at her aunt, but June was smiling broadly at her sister and saying, "You and Carl must come round for dinner, Frances. It's been too long. Alexandra must come, too."

*Did I read her thoughts?* Alex thought in a panic. *Did I hear what she was really thinking?*

At the hotel where the reception was being held, Alex found herself standing next to her uncle Graham, her mother's brother. Graham put his hand on Alex's arm casually and said, "Good to see Grace married, eh, Alex? Tim's a decent chap. I'm sure he'll treat her well." Graham stared at Grace and Tim, who were breezing amongst the guests shaking hands and accepting good wishes. Alex heard Graham's voice in her head say, "grew into a real looker, did Grace. Nice tits. Too prissy, though. Marrying that boring bastard won't do her any good. She needs a real man."

She looked at Graham, who was smiling broadly, still looking at the bride and groom. Alex studied him carefully, trying to will an image into her mind. Nothing happened. She pulled her arm away from his hand.

*Do I see only bad things?* she wondered. *If nothing in particular is going to happen to someone, I don't see it? But I can read people's real thoughts and I can see unhappy futures.*

She took off the hat and studied it carefully. Graham turned to her. "Another drink, Alex?"

"No thanks," she said.

*Is it the hat?* she thought.

*

Over the next week, Alex wore the hat as often as she could. She wore it on the bus on the way to work and looked at the faces of her fellow passengers. The old man at the back of the bus was going to die of hypothermia this winter, undiscovered for days because his grown-up children never visited. The young woman at the front of the bus, juggling a toddler and a baby, was trying to understand why her boyfriend had left her, panicking about how she was going to cope on her own with two kids. When Alex looked into the face of the baby in the young mother's lap, a dreadful image came to her mind: a young woman's body washed up on a riverbank – raped and brutally murdered; newspaper headlines about the hunt for the killer.

Alex worked in the stock room of a catalogue store, spending her days pulling items off shelves and putting them on conveyer belts for customers to collect. It was menial work but she was able to keep to herself. She didn't like any of her colleagues, and suspected they didn't like her much, either. She decided to wear her hat all day to find out what they really thought of her. Damian, the only one who actually bothered to speak to her, thought she was a "stuck-up bitch", she discovered when she brushed past him in the staff kitchen. She could only read people's thoughts, she discovered, when she touched them. Looking at Damian, though, Alex had an image of him bleeding to death outside a night club after a fight. In the image in her mind he was the same age he was now, and he was wearing the black leather jacket he wore to work every day. In most of her images she'd seen people much older.

She wondered about the image she'd seen of herself on the bridge and what this actually meant. *Surely it was a view of what could happen? Was it just a warning of what might happen?* It was true, she'd done stuff before, but that had been a few years ago. She hadn't thought about taking her own life for ages now.

All day she thought about the image she'd seen of Damian. She should try to warn him somehow. Just before closing, she made up her mind to talk to him.

Damian was in conversation with Jack, the two of them snickering. As she approached they turned around and saw her; the look of contempt Damian threw her was unmistakable. They turned their backs to her, snickering louder. Even without touching either of them to know their thoughts, it was clear they were making fun of her.

*Alright then, sod you*, Alex thought angrily, stomping off. *Whatever's going to happen to you, you deserve it, you bastard.*

\*

Two weeks later, Alex turned up to work to find the atmosphere solemn and her colleagues in tears.

"Damian's dead," Cheryl sobbed, when Alex asked her what was going on. "Last night. He was stabbed in the street."

After that, Alex never took the hat off her head. She even slept with it on, tied around her head with a black woollen scarf. It got all bent and out of shape, and it made her hair very greasy, but she didn't really care how strange it looked. She knew things about people she passed in the street that they didn't know themselves. She deduced she was correct in her theory that the hat only showed her bad things that were going to happen, as she never saw any good things. She didn't see visions of everyone she passed in the street. But when she did see visions, she saw murders and suicides and jail sentences, car crashes, heart attacks and cancer deaths. And every time she looked at herself in the mirror, she saw the bridge.

She thought about going back to the shop, to get an explanation from the old lady about what the deal was with this hat, and why it was making her see the future. But she couldn't find the shop again, there was a 'Claire's Accessories' in the place where Alex thought the shop had been. She couldn't remember what the shop had been called, but was sure that wasn't it, and the bag from the shop had no name on it. In the end Alex gave up looking, thinking she must have had the wrong street. It didn't really matter. The hat had given her the ability to see the future, and to hear people's thoughts. How it worked was irrelevant.

One morning she was washing her hair when the doorbell rang. She answered the door with a towel wrapped around her head to find a young man selling kitchen cloths and such things. Alex told him she wasn't interested, and as he turned to go, flashing a warm smile, she saw an image in her mind of the young man as a much older man, collapsing of a heart attack in the middle of the street.

She shut the door and realised with a start that she wasn't wearing the hat. Alex stared at herself in the mirror, studying the towel that was wrapped around her wet hair. The image of the bridge was in her head once more.

She left the hat at home that day, but on the bus going to work, Alex's head was filled with images of death and suicides. She thought about the bridge she kept seeing and realised she knew where it was. Some miles out of London, on the way down to Sussex where her grandparents used to live, there was a river with a big railway bridge. They used to pass it in the car on the way to her grandparents' house. Alex had not been that route for years; her grandparents were both dead now.

The atmosphere at work had been different since Damian's death. No more laughing and joking. Everyone was quiet and solemn. Alex frequently walked into the ladies' toilets to find some colleague or other crying in there. She was feeling bad that she'd not talked to Damian about what was going to happen. He might have been a jerk, but he didn't deserve to die like that. Of course, would he have believed her even if she had said anything? Perhaps it would still have happened anyway. Maybe Damian's destiny had been fixed.

On the day of Damian's funeral, the shop was closed so everyone could go. Alex ransacked her wardrobe for suitable funeral clothes, eventually picking out a long black skirt and a black sweater. She debated wearing the hat – after all, a hat wouldn't be out of place at a funeral, and it was black. But she decided not to. It was getting rather battered and sorry-looking now. She hadn't worn it since the young man selling tea towels had come to the door; she didn't need to any more. She saw the images anyway. She tried to avoid touching people, as when she did so she could hear their thoughts and it was starting to drive her mad. She hadn't had a good night's sleep for weeks; her dreams were full of the images she saw all day, people dying lonely and unpleasant deaths.

When Alex worked Saturdays, she got a day off during the week. About a week after Damian's funeral, she had a Wednesday off. She took the train down to Langford in Sussex, where her grandparents used to live.

She wasn't sure what she was looking for. She got off the train and had a cup of tea in the café at the station, and then wandered around the town aimlessly, plagued with the haunting images of death and destruction that were crowding her brain. She couldn't think about anything else it seemed. Hundreds of images were in her mind, all vying for her attention – people dead and dying, suffering, in pain, or consumed with loneliness and despair.

*So much misery,* she thought. *Everyone's wrapped up their own pain; they all think theirs is worse than everyone else's.*

Alex found herself down by the riverbank, and she followed it for a while before she found the railway bridge. The bridge was a metal criss-cross structure. A hill went up the riverbank on both sides, and the bridge carried the rail straight over the river.

Slinging her bag over her shoulder, Alex began to climb up the hill. It had been raining, and the grass was wet. She climbed carefully, slipping several times. Eventually she found herself standing next to the bridge.

Alex opened her bag and pulled out the hat. It was grubby and out of shape now, but she clamped it onto her head nonetheless. The brim, squashed and crumpled, was coming away and half of it dangled over Alex's face pathetically.

The kaleidoscope of images in her head became more intense when she put the hat on. Faces of family members and strangers, swirling and spinning in her mind; gradually growing louder, a cacophony of wailing and crying, a symphony of human suffering.

Alex pulled her bag off her shoulder and set it down on the ground, before turning to the bridge. A narrow ledge ran along the side. Purposefully she stepped onto it, pulling herself along using the metal cross rails on the side of the bridge.

It seemed to take a long time for Alex to make her way to the centre, the noise and images in her head getting louder and more vivid all the while.

When she reached the centre she stopped, turning herself around carefully. Holding onto the side of the bridge with both hands she stood staring down at the murky water far below. The sharp edge of the bridge cut into the soles of her feet; the rusted metal bars of the sides were cold and gritty beneath her sweaty palms. She could feel flakes of paint peeling off and sticking to her skin.

*You can't change the future*, Alex thought. *I understand now. We all have a destiny.* For a moment she hung there, staring down at the black swirling water, reflecting on the faces in her head

Then she let go, and plummeted forward. Falling down, down, towards the black water.

# Morgan's Father

It is late when Morgan leaves the cemetery. She did not mean to be out so long but has lost track of time. The street is deserted and silent. She pulls her coat tightly about herself and starts for home. Her thoughts are of her father.

She thinks of him stroking her hair as she sits in his lap, the whiskers on his chin scratching her face as he holds her close. "If any one ever hurts you, Morgan, you tell me," he whispers to her. "I'll go after him. I won't let anyone hurt my girl."

He is a big and bulky man, with the strength of a heavyweight wrestler and a temper to match. Except with Morgan. He has never spoken a word in anger to her, never treated her with anything but love and tenderness.

Morgan and her father have always been a team. Together forever. She looks like him, with her dark dishevelled hair and deep green eyes. He is the teacher, she the willing pupil, learning all the skills and secrets he can show her. As long as she and her father are together, Morgan knows she is safe.

Her pace quickens. She must get home. She must get back to her father, back to safety.

Not a single car passes as she makes her way home. She doesn't know what time it is; she never wears a watch.

She is passing the business estate on the corner of the street she lives on. It looks dark and foreboding so late at night. From the corner of her eye she thinks she sees something move in the shadows. *My imagination*, she thinks uneasily, and quickens her pace.

A moment later she slows down, growing nervous. She is sure she hears footsteps echoing hers. She knows it is a man, even though she cannot make out his face in the darkness. She clutches her shoulder bag tighter to her; steps up her pace. The echoing footsteps behind her also increase in speed. The man is closing in on her. She walks even faster. The footsteps still match hers. She begins to jog, then to run.

The man is right behind her; a strong arm grabs her roughly around the neck. She tries to scream but the man clamps a hand over her mouth. She feels the grip loosen slightly, then something cold and hard is pressed to her throat. She knows it is a knife; she can feel the pain of the blade tip pressing through her skin.

"Money." The voice is harsh and guttural. "I want money."

"I-I haven't got any money," Morgan stammers.

The man spins her round, keeps the knife pressed to her throat, one arm pulls on her bag as he yanks her into the courtyard of the silent office block.

"The bag. Give it to me."

Morgan slides her bag down her arm and holds it out to the man. He lets go of her arm to grab it. As he moves, his face is illuminated by a nearby streetlamp. A hard, weather-beaten face, lined and pitted with scars; his hair, poking out from beneath a black woollen hat, is greying and curly, his eyes dark and flashing hatred. In the brief moment he moves his hand to take her bag Morgan screeches and lunges at him, trying to wrench the knife from his grasp.

She throws herself at him, knocking him off balance. They both fall to the floor and struggle wildly, the man releasing a string of savage curses. He stabs blindly with the knife but misses. Morgan scratches his face with her long nails, pokes his eyes, pulls off his hat.

The man throws a punch at Morgan which catches her across the jaw. She screams and falls backwards. He scrabbles to his feet and runs away, taking the shoulder bag with him.

Morgan is stunned. By the time she gets to her feet, feeling her bruised face gingerly, the man has long gone. She has his blood under her fingernails and his woolly hat in her hand.

It takes Morgan only a few minutes to get home. Tears of rage brim in her green eyes. The bag contains nothing of value, save for a few pounds, but the thought of that animal pawing her personal things fills her with fury.

She gets to her house, fumbling in her pockets for the key (never has she been so thankful she doesn't keep it in her bag), and stumbles into the hallway.

She pauses at the foot of the stairs to light a candle on the stand there. She carries it with her into the living room.

The living room, decorated in a stark black and red colour scheme, contains dozens more candles, standing on the window sill, the shelves, the mantelpiece. Morgan lights each one in turn from the candle she holds in her hand.

Above the mantelpiece hangs a mirror. Morgan stares thoughtfully into it for a moment, the glow from the flickering candles casting odd shadows across her injured face. With the middle finger of her left hand she traces the swelling purple bruise disfiguring the line of her jaw, and the drops of blood that are drying in the corner of her mouth. A scowl crosses her face and she turns away from the mirror.

The candles in the room are a variety of colours – black, white, red, blue, purple, yellow, green. Morgan selects three and carries them to the low coffee table in the centre of the room.

She studies her hands. Blood from her attacker has dried in flakes under her fingernails. She spends a moment picking out as much as she can, balancing the flakes in the palm of her right hand. With her left she pulls the attacker's hat out of her coat pocket.

She turns the hat upside down and shakes the flakes of blood from the palm of her hand into it. She carries the hat to the table, where a glass sphere about the size of a melon sits on an iron stand. Morgan covers the glass sphere with the hat.

She closes her eyes and sits still for a moment, whispering under her breath.

Her eyes snap open. Heavy footsteps tramp up the cellar steps. Morgan hears the cellar door creak, and feels a momentary blast of cold air from the hallway. The door slams shut.

"Hello, Father," Morgan says as the bulky figure steps into the room.

"Morgan," growls the figure in a low voice. Morgan's father moves slowly, with a limping gait, as he crosses the room. He sits down in an armchair and stares intently at Morgan. "You got hurt," he says finally.

"I got mugged, Father." Morgan's hands move to her face. "He hit me, and made off with my bag. Do you see what he did to me?" She raises one of the candles to cast more light on her face.

"Yes," her father says. His expression is impassive, his eyes unblinking, as he stares at Morgan's face. "I see."

"I want you to go after him, Father. I want you to punish him for what he did to me. I can show you what he looks like." She lifts the hat off the crystal sphere. Through the swirling mist that materialises in the glass, a face appears. A grizzled face, pitted with lines and scars.

Morgan looks at her father. "Can you find him for me, Father?"

Her father nods slowly. "Of course, Morgan."

He gets up and shuffles across the room. Morgan follows him into the hallway. He stops, waits expectantly. She opens the door for him, watches him go limping down the path, down the road. She shuts the door behind him. As she heads back down the hallway, she stops for a moment in front of the doorway that leads to the cellar from whence her father came. She smiles to herself.

*

Jack sits in the park with a torch, going through his booty in a very black mood. *The bitch was wearing expensive-looking stuff, she should have had something of value on her.*

The contents of the bag lie scattered at his feet, where he has tossed them in disgust. The amount of junk women haul around with them in their bags never ceases to amaze him. Sometimes there are bonuses like mobile phones, MP3 players, cameras. Usually there is at least some jewellery, debit cards (with the PIN number written handily in a diary or an address book close by), something he could use or sell or get money from somehow. This bitch has nothing. A few scribbled-in notebooks, a couple of lipsticks (bright red), and less than twenty quid in cash. Not even a decent leather purse; she keeps her money in a scruffy plastic wallet.

*What a bleeding waste of time.* He tosses the bag over his shoulder carelessly.

He could hang about for someone else, he supposes, but it's getting really late. How many more stupid women would he find wandering about alone at this time of night? Better to give up, go back to the hovel he calls home, get some shut-eye.

As he sits pondering his decision, not really feeling like getting up and walking home (he could always sleep here on the bench), he is suddenly startled by the sound of movement close by. He brightens; perhaps there are more pickings to be had after all.

He looks around. He sees a figure moving across the park; a limping, shuffling gait like someone who has arthritis or a bad leg. A man, Jack decides, and a big man at that. But if he's lame, then perhaps ...?

Jack remains on his bench, wondering if the man has seen him yet. He comes closer. Although he is still some distance away, a sickening smell is wafting over to Jack from the figure's direction. A tramp, then. So not worth the effort.

The figure appears to be moving in his direction. Jack continues to watch as it gets closer, intrigued as to where the tramp is going. Perhaps he wants to mug me, Jack thinks, and the thought strikes him as highly amusing.

The figure is less than ten feet away now, shrouded in darkness. The smell is much stronger, overpowering, and Jack suddenly wants to retch. He gets up, intending to move as far away from the tramp as possible. He is held by a wave of nausea.

Suddenly the figure is upon him. Jack turns the torch around, to get a better look at who is approaching, and what he sees roots him to the spot in fear. It is not a man towering over him but a walking corpse, a putrid half-skeleton, flesh hanging in tatters from discoloured bones, eyes nothing but empty sockets, rotten intestines hanging out of the hole that used to be its stomach. The thing stretches out skeletal hands, strips of putrid flesh dropping off bones every time it moves.

Jack wants to scream, he wants to run: He finds he is unable to move. The torch falls out of his hands and clatters to the ground.

The thing twists what is left of its face into the mockery of a grin. "For Morgan," it rasps from the depths of what was once its throat.

*

The next morning, her father safely tucked up in his bed in the cellar, Morgan smiles over the newspaper headline as she eats her breakfast. THIRD HEADLESS CORPSE FOUND IN SOUTH PARK: POLICE STILL BAFFLED.

She folds up the paper and drinks her tea. She thinks about what special treat she can prepare for her father. After all, he deserves a big thank you. He brought her a lovely trophy for her collection last night.

# Train To Maladomini

Darkness. Pain. A sense of ... nothingness. Endless pain.

Somewhere out of the darkness came an awareness of existence.

Jake opened his eyes. Blinding light pierced his pupils, and he raised a hand to shield his eyes. After a moment he tried exposing them to the light again, slowly letting them adjust.

How long had he been asleep? He couldn't remember. Vague memories swirled round his head, memories of faces, someone screaming ... a long time ago. He had a dim recollection of pain, terrible pain. He couldn't feel pain now.

His eyes had started to focus, and he could make out a face directly opposite, the withered face of an old man with paper-thin skin and long strands of wispy white hair. His strikingly pale blue eyes seemed, somehow, to be even older.

"So," the old man said, an amused expression crossing his face, "young Jake joins us at last."

Jake tried to speak, but his throat felt dry. He couldn't make any words come out. He nodded vaguely. He tried to take in his surroundings. He appeared to be in a train carriage, but something about it didn't seem right. The interior was painted completely black, and the windows were small grimy squares. He had absolutely no recollection of how he got here.

"You are wondering, perhaps, who I am?" the old man said. "This man who knows your name. You do not know me, but I know you. I have been waiting to meet you for a long time. You may call me Baal."

Jake felt that perhaps his vocal chords had finally woken up. "Bale," he croaked. "Strange sort of name. Is it foreign, or something?"

"Foreign, certainly, to the world you know," the old man replied.

"If you know so much, how about telling me where the hell I am?" Jake said.

The old man looked amused. "If you do not know, perhaps you should try to remember where you were?"

Jake rubbed his eyes. His head felt like it was stuffed with cotton wool. "I can't remember much of anything. I think there was a party ... there must have been a party." Any time he woke up feeling this rough, there had always been a party. Not that he could remember much about them.

He managed to pin down a memory that was less vague than the others – a face, a girl's face. Pretty, blonde, laughing a lot. Good, that was a start. He focused on her face, tried to expand on it. She wore a sexy red dress. He remembered being more interested in her body than her face. What was her name? She had never told him.

Trying to remember any more was like wading through quicksand, memories struggling furiously but sinking fast. His head was starting to ache from the effort. He rubbed his temples wearily. How the hell had he ended up on this train? He looked out of the window, and could see nothing but swirling grey fog.

"Where is this train headed?" Jake asked.

The old man smiled. "That depends on where you expect to be going."

"Just what the fuck is that supposed to mean? I expect to wake up in a bed of some sort with a naked blonde lying beside me. If I woke up face down in the gutter, at least I'd be able to work out what had happened."

There was something that deeply disturbed Jake in the old man's eyes. To avoid looking at them, he studied the train carriage more carefully. There were no aisles in the carriage, he noticed; the bench he sat on ran right from one end of the carriage to the other. The bench the old man sat on ran parallel. He could see only one other person. At the opposite side of the train, on Jake's bench, a dishevelled young woman sat, slumped over. She appeared to be asleep.

The carriage was full of such rows of benches, but Jake couldn't make out whether or not there were other people on them. He tried to stand, for a better look, but he could not move. As he looked down at himself he realised in horror that black iron chains anchored his legs and body to the seat, leaving only his arms free. "What the hell's going on?" he demanded. "Who's tied me to the fucking seat?"

The old man spread his arms, revealing that he, too, was draped in chains. "Look," he said, pointing a claw-like finger out of the window.

It felt to Jake like the train was stopping. The steady clack-clacking of the wheels on the track were slowing in tempo. He peered through the filthy window, and saw that the fog had cleared. The train was coming to a stop by a platform. Jake strained to see some clue that might tell him where he was. He caught a glimpse of the sign on the station platform: ELESYIUM.

"Let me get off," Jake said, panic rising in his voice. "Let me off now!"

"You can't get off," the old man said simply.

Out of the window, Jake could see the people who had just got off the train wandering about aimlessly on the platform, looking dazed and disorientated. Beyond the platform lay a land of lush green fields and trees. Nobody, from what Jake could see, was carrying any luggage.

"What do you mean I can't get off? Get me off this fucking train now!"

The train began to move again, away from the platform and back into the impenetrable grey fog.

"Even if there were no chains," Baal explained, "you would discover that there are no doors. You cannot get off the train."

"What is this shit? I got on; how the fuck do I get off?"

"You got on the same way they did." The old man indicated the other end of the bench. The girl Jake had noticed earlier had woken up. She clutched at the chains around her waist with wide, unfocused eyes. Along each forearm were the railroad punctures of the heroin addict. Sitting opposite the girl was a thin, middle-aged bearded man, staring unseeing at the nothingness out of the window. The cuffs of his shirt were stained with blood, and he had red gashes in both wrists. What disturbed Jake most, however, was the fact that the man had not been there a moment ago.

"I can't remember getting on!" Jake cried, getting frightened. "I don't even know where the hell I am. I want to get off, now!"

"If you think, Jake, you will know exactly where you are. Concentrate, and remember. Remember how you got here."

*Okay*, Jake thought. *Be calm. Panicking won't work. Think. Think.* He shut his eyes, and tried to remember. His mind turned over and over frantically; he forced himself to focus on the one thing he could remember clearly, the blonde girl at the party.

The party. He remembered the girl hanging on his arm. She was so drunk she could barely stand up. He remembered he'd been chatting her up, and she kept falling over, pressing against him, giggling. He took her out of the house, down the path, holding her up most of the way. He was having trouble walking himself. He seemed to remember someone shouting to him about not wanting him to drive.

He didn't listen, of course. He reached his car, opened the door, bundled the girl in. She fell across the seat, tried to pick herself up. The short skirt of her dress hitched itself up to her waist. She was wearing transparent black pants underneath, and suddenly Jake didn't want to wait to get all the way back to his place; he wanted to get to a quiet bit of road as quickly as possible and get down to business.

He couldn't remember any more after that. Just vague sensations. Screaming. Shattering glass. And terrible pain.

An accident. It hit him suddenly with astounding clarity. He'd trashed his car. He had a sudden, flash image, the girl lying sprawled across the passenger seat, impaled by a long, twisted shard of metal.

Jake looked down at his trembling hands, pale, pale hands. He ran them slowly over his torn leather jacket, parted the lapels, studied the shirt underneath. It was ripped in places, and stained with blood. He pulled at the collar, tried to see his chest. It was scored with great bloodied welts. Yet there was no pain, not now.

He looked up at the old man, who gazed at him, expressionless. "Am I dead?" he asked quietly.

"Well, the penny drops at last," Baal replied.

"But ... what is this place?"

"Most would call it the afterlife. But, since you don't believe in the afterlife, you can call it what you like."

"But a train? A fucking train that chugs along dropping people off in heaven?"

"There are some people on this train who will get off at one of the many layers of heaven. We just passed Elysium, as you saw."

"But there are no doors!" Jake could feel panic rising in his chest.

"There are no doors in this carriage," the old man said. "Why would you be getting off at Elysium? You don't believe in heaven, remember? Do you think they'd have you anyway?

Besides the drinking and the gambling you have, after all, killed three people in your short and repulsive life."

"I did time for all those," Jake protested, and suddenly wondered why he felt the need to defend himself, here, for things that had happened such a long time ago.

"For a couple of bar-room brawls that became too violent, perhaps justice has been served. But what about the child who died because you were too drunk to figure out where the road ended and the pavement began? Do you think a few months in jail and a driving ban, which you ignored anyway, was punishment enough?"

"Who the fuck are you, old man?"

"Who I am is not important; you will learn in time. I am simply here to make sure you realise your reward in the afterlife will reflect your behaviour in life."

"Are you saying I'm going to hell? This is some demon train, taking me to hell?"

"There are different levels of hell also, Jake. Surely you can figure it out. What sort of torment and suffering can you imagine in which to spend the rest of eternity? You are chained to a bench, unable to move, in a train whose length is infinite, able to do nothing but watch other people disembark and head for beautiful places you will never be a part of? All of eternity, Jake. Do you have any concept of how long that is? You are not going to hell, my friend. You are here already."

The old man pointed his long-fingernailed hand up to the ceiling. Jake found himself involuntarily looking up. Emblazoned across the ceiling in large red letters was a single word: MALADOMINI.

"Make yourself comfortable, Jake. You'll be here for a long time." The old man vanished suddenly. His hideous cackling laughter rung in Jake's ears for much longer, emphasising the endless clacking of the train as it rumbled down the track, the track it would travel for all eternity.

# The Boy With Blue Eyes

It was on the Victoria line that I first set eyes on him, somewhere between Green Park and Oxford Circus. It was a Monday in September. The day started out like any other. It was quarter past eight in the morning as I shuffled across Victoria station concourse. Not fully awake, I allowed myself to be carried along by a surge of fellow commuters heading to the underground station.

As usual, the platform was crowded. I plodded to the right side of the platform and waited. Three full trains went past before I even attempted to board one. I squeezed onto the fourth train and deposited myself between the seats. Someone sitting close by got up and squeezed past me to get off. I pounced on the empty seat, and sat down before someone else could beat me to it.

I turned to the recruitment ads in my copy of *The Metro*. As usual I was looking for a new job. I'd spent the best part of my working life hating whatever job I had at the time and seeking out something better – only the one that seems better on paper never proves to be that way after a few months in the job.

Then I got the feeling that someone was looking at me. I peered over the top of my newspaper and my gaze locked onto a pair of devastatingly beautiful eyes. They were the brightest blue I had ever seen. The colour of the sea on a summer's day. Wide and clear and bright eyes, staring right into mine.

I felt a fluttering in the pit of my stomach, and my knees began to tremble. Flustered, I folded my hands in my lap and tore my gaze away from those entrancing eyes, to check out the body they resided in. He was young, maybe twenty, with a face that could have belonged to a member of any boy band. Unblemished pale skin. Lips that were pink and full. Slightly asymmetrical nose. The eyelashes that framed those gorgeous blue eyes were as long and thick as a girl's. His hair was short and light brown, tousled by the wind outside. He wore khaki combat trousers, hiking boots, a black T-shirt emblazoned with an Iron Maiden logo, and a faded denim jacket. On his lips hovered the shadow of a smile as he watched me. Even from that I could see the smile that he was capable of, and knew right then that if he were to flash that smile on me fully, my legs would become water and my heart would burst right out of my chest.

Then we stopped at Oxford Circus, the doors opened, and he got off the train.

The doors slammed shut and the train moved again, carrying me and hundreds of other passengers onwards to work.

I sat there and my mind was full of snow, like a TV screen without reception. I felt like a part of me had walked out of the train with the blue-eyed boy and that my life would never be the same again.

*

I carried on going through the motions of the usual routine for the rest of the week. Taking the underground to Kings Cross every morning to get to the office. Back home to my flat in Streatham, which I shared with my best friend Susan. Susan and I had been friends since school. We got on best when we were both single – when we were able to spend Friday nights at the pub and Saturday nights clubbing together, drinking far too much and checking out the men who looked like they might be on the pull.

When one of us had a boyfriend and the other didn't, that's when we were furthest apart. That was how it was that week. Susan had been seeing Scott for a month. I'd finished with Rob two weeks earlier. Rob was tall, blonde, charming and solvent, and as I had discovered rather too late, completely incapable of being monogamous. We'd been seeing each other for three months when I found out he was also seeing another woman. During the argument that followed, he insisted that he'd never claimed at any time he would be seeing me exclusively, and I had clearly been interpreting things to be more serious than they were.

Perhaps he had a point. Rob and I had enjoyed many trips to the cinema, countless nights of great sex, two weekend jaunts to the country in posh hotels where we saw nothing beyond the bedroom door. He'd never specifically said I was the only woman in his life, but neither had he mentioned there were others. Perhaps I had been assuming. Perhaps this was my mistake with men. I wanted commitment, when all they wanted was a bit of fun.

After I broke up with Rob, all my friends took great pleasure in telling me what they had always thought of him. It appeared that he'd made at least one pass at every one of my girl friends, something I wasn't aware of when I was seeing him. Rob wasn't merely a two-timer; there were probably at least three or four women he was juggling at any one time. He was a man wanting a good time. So he was unable to make a commitment. Was it so wrong for me to expect one?

On Friday that week Scott was out of town, and Susan and I had a night at the pub. We eyed up the men and chatted about clothes and sex and so on – almost like old times.

I told Susan about the boy on the train, whose eyes had not left my memory since I first discovered him looking at me.

"I wish I could be so lucky," Susan said. "I never see any gorgeous men on the underground."

"I can still see his face in my mind," I said. "He looked at me. He must have known I was staring at him."

"So maybe he fancied you."

"But he got off the train."

"Yeah, that's what people do. Eight o'clock in the morning, everyone's on their way to work. Just part of the rat race. You saw a tasty piece who smiled at you, and it's made your week. Just a small pleasure in the daily grind of life."

I couldn't find a way to tell her that it was more than that. The memory of the boy gnawed away inside me like a hunger, and I felt like I was going crazy with it.

The following day Scott came and took Susan away for the rest of the weekend. I was left alone with the cat until Monday, obliged to face the reality of how lonely existence can be when you are single.

*

I dreamed about those eyes every night. Not a morning passed I didn't wake up with an image of the boy's face in my mind. It was as if it was permanently imprinted behind my retinas. The dreams became more and more explicit. First of all the dreams just involved the boy sitting on the train, exactly the way I had seen him. Then the dreams changed, and each night they would get more involved and more explicit. He was walking towards me, that deadly smile on his face, taking off his denim jacket and his T-shirt. The next time he was leaning over me, his muscled torso glistening with sweat, and I reached up and ran my hands over the firm flesh of his body, my fingers trembling at the texture of his skin. Then the dream became a fully-fledged erotic fantasy, and I awoke drenched with sweat, my limbs trembling, feeling a need for him so urgent it consumed my thoughts.

I had to find this boy again.

*

At the end of the following week – eleven days after I had first seen the boy – I saw him again.

I got on the underground at Victoria as usual, and as there were no seats I hung onto a pole by the door. I scanned the occupants of the carriage and there he was, sitting in the middle of the carriage. He wore black jeans, a plain white T-shirt and the same faded denim jacket. He had a denim rucksack in his lap. He was reading a copy of *Empire* magazine.

He got up at Oxford Circus and brushed past me to get off the train. He did not see me this time, but as he passed by his shoulder touched my right arm, which I was using to hang on to the bar at the top of the carriage.

It felt like a surge of electricity had coursed through my body. I couldn't stop shaking. I watched him walk up the platform, staring at the way his backside moved in the tight jeans. As the doors of the train were about to close, I was suddenly seized by the impulse to leap out of the carriage and follow him.

It was a foolish thought, of course. I would be late for work, and how could I possibly hope to keep track of him as he mingled with the rush hour crowd heading out of the station?

Nevertheless, that's what I found myself doing. I pushed through the crowd, desperately trying to keep sight of the boy as he went through the barriers and turned into Oxford Street.

I caught a glimpse of him heading down Oxford Street towards Tottenham Court Road and hurried to keep up.

I was caught up in the surge of the crowd, trying desperately to see over heads taller than mine. He was ahead of me now, and lost in the thick fog of commuters heading to work, with briefcases or coffee cups – and sometimes both – clamped in their hands. I couldn't see the boy in the throng, and my heart sank. I'd lost him.

Then the crowd pushed me past HMV and there he was, talking to someone outside. As I moved closer, desperately trying to keep them in sight, they disappeared inside the store.

It was too early for the store to be open, so he had to work there. A sense of relief flooded through me. At least I knew where he was going to be all day. The question was, now that I had that knowledge, what was I going to do with it?

I walked down the street past HMV to McDonald's, where I nursed a watery coffee and a lukewarm Sausage McMuffin for three quarters of an hour. Then I walked around trying to find a quiet place to use my mobile. I had to walk a long way. Eventually I ended up down at the end of one of the side streets off Tottenham Court Road and called the office, desperately hoping a car wouldn't go by. I was making out I was sick. The sound of a car engine would blow my cover.

Fortunately my boss was not at his desk. I always think it's much easier to lie to voicemail than it is to lie in person. I put on my best croaky voice. "Hi Rick, this is Shelley. I won't be in today because I'm not feeling well. I guess I'll probably be okay by Monday, so I'll see you then. 'Bye."

By the time I got back to HMV it was nearly 10 o'clock and the Oxford Street shopping frenzy had started. The fact that HMV is a huge store was a mixed blessing. On the positive side, by moving through the different departments I was able to hang around without buying anything or attracting the attention of the security staff. On the minus side, there were a lot of staff in the shop and I could not see the blue-eyed boy.

I worked my way methodically through each department, pretending to browse. Chart CDs. Classical music. Computer games. DVDs. All the while I was trying to work out what to do when I did see him. Staring at him hungrily with my mouth open was simply not going to impress. But I hadn't really thought about what should happen next. Logically, I supposed, I should ask him out on a date. Was this what I really wanted? Yes, naturally. I fancied him, didn't I?

Actually it was more than that. He set my soul on fire. He'd aroused in me a longing the likes of which I had never experienced before. And I had not even met him. I had caught sight of him for a few seconds on a train, and it had been enough to turn me into a gibbering wreck.

But I did not dwell on that thought too long. I made up my mind that when I saw him, I would suggest meeting him for dinner.

Then I saw him. He was in the T-shirts section stacking some Simpsons T-shirts in the rack. He still wore his black jeans, but he was now wearing a standard staff-issue HMV top. From where I stood I could see his profile. His lips were parted slightly as he concentrated, his brow furrowed slightly.

He must have sensed me staring at him, for he turned and focused those too-blue eyes on me. He smiled. "Hi," he said.

I felt like I was about to faint, and used an arm to steady myself against the wall. I know how corny it sounds, but I felt as though I was in the presence of an angel. I could feel my legs trembling.

"Can I help you?" the boy said. The sound of his voice sent fresh thrills down my spine – it was deep and throaty, the dialect lazy with a twinge of East London. He was still smiling. I opened my mouth, and found my voice had completely deserted me.

"You look familiar," he said, frowning a little. "Have we met?"

*In my dreams this past week and a half. You've been making love to me, your skin slick with sweat, your chest moving under my hands as I touch you in the throes of climax...*

I finally found my voice. "I've seen you on the underground," I croaked. It didn't actually sound like my voice; it sounded like it was on loan from Louis Armstrong.

"Oh, is that it?" the boy said brightly. The shadow of a smile danced on his lips. He was waiting for me to speak, but something in his face (God, the blue of those eyes, how can anything mortal have eyes that colour?) suggested that perhaps he knew exactly what I wanted.

"Erm ..." I gathered my courage from deep within and steeled myself. I had to do this now or I would go crazy. "I know this might sound a little forward, since we don't know each other, but I would like to know you better and I was hoping you'd let me take you out to dinner. Sometime. Maybe."

His expression did not change at all. He didn't even blink. He still wore that knowing half-smile on his face. A long moment passed before he spoke. "What about tonight?"

"To-tonight?" I stammered, stunned.

"Sure, why not? I haven't got anything else on."

I managed to steady my shaking legs. "Tonight will be fine."

"You know the Glassblower, by Piccadilly Circus?"

I nodded.

"How about I meet you there?" he said. "Downstairs. About six-thirty."

"That will be fine," I said.

"Okay then. Look forward to it."

"Okay," I said. I was trying not to stare at those startling eyes, but I couldn't help it.

"I do have to get back to work now," he said apologetically.

"Oh yes. I'm sorry. I'll see you tonight then."

I left the store, but I was at a loss what to do next. My goal had been achieved – he had agreed to see me tonight.

I checked my watch. It was nearly half past twelve. Six hours till I could see him again. I thought I should get some lunch but, in spite of eating nothing since the insubstantial McMuffin, I was not hungry. My stomach was doing excited flip-flops. Besides, I had a dinner date. I ought to allow myself to get hungry enough for a meal tonight.

I headed back to Victoria and got on a train back to Streatham. I let myself into the empty flat, dumped my belongings in the hallway and took a long hot shower. After that I took a long time trying to decide what to wear. I would never be able to explain to anyone just how important this date was. This was possibly the most important date in the history of the world. How could anything in my modest wardrobe possibly be right for that?

I eventually decided on my black leather mini-skirt, black tights and a black sleeveless T-shirt, which had a v-neck and exposed a lot of cleavage. By this point there was a sizeable pile of clothes on the floor of my room where I'd discarded them after trying them on and deciding they weren't right. I blow-dried my hair and fluffed it out with mousse and styling spritz. I painted my fingernails bright red. I applied some make-up. I chose a lipstick that matched my nail varnish.

Finally I zipped my feet into knee-high black leather boots, put on my black woollen coat, picked up my hand bag, and searched for my keys.

I walked back to the station and got on a train to Victoria. I couldn't concentrate on anything. I saw the beautiful boy's face everywhere I looked – on the train display board, in the window of every carriage as the train rolled by. Those true blue eyes were burning into my soul.

It was half past five by the time I got to the pub. It was already starting to fill up with office workers celebrating the start of the weekend. It was going to be very busy later.

I got myself a bottle of Beck's and found an empty table where I had a good view of the door. I sat down to wait.

It was quarter to seven when he turned up. By that time I was on my third Beck's. I had tried to make my beer last as long as possible – already nervous and drinking on an empty stomach, I did not want to be embarrassingly pissed by the time he arrived.

The thought that he might not turn up at all had crossed my mind several times. After all, he didn't know me from Adam – I could be a complete loon for all he knew. I had been staring at him quite intently. Perhaps he thought I was crazy and had said whatever it took to get me to go away and leave him alone. I did not know what I would have done if he had stood me up. An image came to mind – me climbing over the railings of Tower Bridge, falling into the cold, cold water below. It was an amazingly soothing image. However, I didn't know whether the Thames was deep enough – or cold enough – in which to drown oneself. It would be very embarrassing to attempt to commit suicide and fail, I reflected. If you're going to do it, do it right the first time.

At that moment he walked in the door, saving me from further thoughts of suicide. The room temperature seemed to go up twenty degrees as he closed the door behind him. He was wearing the same T-shirt I had seen him in on the tube this morning, and carried his rucksack slung carelessly over one shoulder. I waved my bottle of Becks at him frantically. He saw me, waved, and came over to my table.

"Hi." He dumped his pack down by the side of the table, gesturing at my drink as he sat down. "Ready for another one?"

"Why not?" I replied. I watched him walk to the bar – again enjoying the view – and wondered about this overwhelming sense of joy that he had brought to me simply by walking through the door. My heart was singing. It sounds like a stupid thing to say, but it's how it felt. I ached to lose myself in those blue eyes. To disappear into his arms forever, and never have to face the world again.

By the time we finished our drinks the pub was very crowded, so we left and took a walk down to Trafalgar Square. He walked with a loping gait, his back pack slung over one shoulder. I looped my arm through his, basking in the presence of him, the musky smell, enveloping myself in the aura of joy he was generating around me.

He was pretty quiet and didn't say a lot. I was aware that I was doing most of the talking. I was saying anything, to cover my nervousness – most of it was gibberish. Throughout the course of the evening I told him about my flat in Streatham, about my cat, about Susan – and for some unknown reason I told him about Rob.

We ended up having dinner at The Spaghetti House in St Martin's Lane. Nothing special, but because I hadn't made reservations anywhere, we had to go someplace where there was a table free.

There was never any conversation about whether we were going to have sex – I knew that it was my intention from the first moment I saw him, and I can only assume he realised that, because the itinerary of the night just seemed to happen without any discussion.

By eleven we had checked into a seedy hotel on the outskirts of Soho – the sort of place where you can rent a room by the hour. I have no doubt that most of the clientele in the place consisted of prostitutes and their customers, but at that stage I didn't care. Going home would have taken too long; I couldn't wait any more.

The room was shabby, the toilet didn't flush properly, the bed was small and creaky, and the sheets were soiled. But I barely noticed any of these things. By the time we left the restaurant I had been consumed by those too-blue eyes, and my desire was so strong it was a physical pain.

*

It felt like we fucked for hours. I don't usually use that word to describe sex but, in this case, that's just what it was. It couldn't be described as making love; that phrase is associated with tenderness and affection. That wasn't what happened with us.

The sex was raw, primitive and animal. It also blew my mind. It was far and away the best sex I had ever had.

I told him this afterwards, as we lay naked in the lumpy bed amongst soiled sheets, sharing a joint he had rolled up.

He just smiled and said, "practice makes perfect."

"Oh? And so what number notch on the bed post am I?"

"I lost count a long time ago."

"I've had seven lovers. Eight including you. I was fifteen when I gave up the cherry – to a spotty youth called Michael Ellis who I thought I was in love with. I wasn't, of course. I just thought I was then. Once he had his way, he promptly dumped me for a dumb blonde who was a year older than me, and about three cup sizes bigger. So, eight lovers in ten years. Less than one a year. What's the average, these days?"

"Don't ask me about averages. By the time I was fifteen there'd been so many I had already lost track."

"So how old were you when you started sowing the oats, if you'd lost track by fifteen?"

He smiled. "Twelve."

"You're kidding. How old was she?"

"Twenty-six. She was my teacher."

"You're having me on."

"Why would I lie?" he said mildly.

"You could be trying to impress me," I said uncertainly.

"I've just met you and we've been rolling around all night. What would I gain from impressing you now?"

I said nothing. His words disturbed me. He carried on with his tale, apparently unperturbed. "I do remember that first time, though. I had a crush on this teacher, you see. Every time I sat in her class and watched her writing sums on the board, I imagined her naked and it gave me a stiffie. I tried not to think about it, but it only made it worse. Then one day she caught me playing with myself, and kept me behind after class. 'That's not a polite thing to do in public,' she said. 'I can't help it,' I told her. 'You turn me on. It's driving me crazy.'"

"You really said that to your teacher?"

"Yes. She took me out to McDonald's and bought me a cheeseburger and a vanilla milkshake. Then she drove me back to her house and shagged me."

"No way."

"She said to me, afterwards, that I mustn't tell anyone what had happened, or she'd get the sack. I wasn't about to say a word. I mean, I fancied her like crazy and couldn't believe my luck. I didn't want to get her into trouble. But either someone found out, or I wasn't the first schoolboy she'd shagged, because two weeks later I went to school one day and she had gone. We had a new teacher carrying on as if nothing had happened, and no one ever mentioned her again. But after that, I knew I had something. I've never had to go chasing after any woman for a fuck. They come to me. Like you did. I'm hardly going to turn any away, am I?"

"What, any woman that comes on to you you'll shag? Even if you don't fancy her?"

"I've never met a woman I didn't fancy. I like women. I've had them fat and thin, black, white, Oriental, Christian, Muslim, Jewish. You name it. I've had a few deaf ones, and once, one who only had one leg."

"Have you ever had a blind woman?"

"No." He gazed at me intently. "It's all visual, you see. Women who see me, want to shag me."

As I swam in those blue, blue eyes, I had no doubt that he was being deadly serious.

"The teacher said to me, 'you're going to break a lot of hearts when you get older'," he said. "But I don't think I do. I don't ask for ties, or commitment. I just like a good time. They all know that."

I lay with my head propped on my elbow, getting lost in those vivid blue eyes. "Have you ever considered modelling? A face like yours could make a lot of money."

He snorted derisively. "No way. I don't want to be tied down like that, sucked into a seamy underworld and committed to all sorts of contracts and promises. I want to be free. To go as I please. And come." He smiled lazily. A thrill ran down my spine as I looked at that devastating smile.

"What about the job at HMV?"

He shrugged. "That's just casual work. I work for whoever will pay me, I leave when I've got enough money to eat for a while. When the money runs out I just look for work someplace else. A man can always find work if he looks hard enough."

"Why is it all men are so afraid of commitment?"

"I didn't say all men were. It doesn't suit me."

"What if you were to meet someone you fell in love with?"

"I'm not sure I believe in love. I think it's a fantasy two people choose to believe in when they're afraid of being alone. Being alone has never worried me. It can be nice to have company, and I love sex. But sometimes it's nice to be alone, too. And when I don't want to be alone anymore, there's never a shortage of women."

Eventually we stopped talking and I fell asleep, in the warm embrace of his arms.

*

When I woke up, to the sound of police sirens outside, he was gone. I scrabbled for my watch; it was ten o'clock. His side of the bed was cold and rumpled; he must have been gone for some hours. I looked for a note, but he hadn't left one.

I managed to coax enough water from the ancient and tarnished shower head for a lukewarm and unsatisfactory shower. As I dried off in the cold and mildew-stained bathroom, using the stained and threadbare towel provided by the hotel, it occurred to me that in the hours I had spent with my blue-eyed boy, he had never told me his name.

*

That night was the last time I had a full night's sleep. In my dreams I replay our night of sex, over and over again, my mind trying vainly to recapture the feelings of that night, the untempered passion that we shared. I wake up in the middle of the night in a sweat, seeing his face fading into view before me, those blue eyes shining in the darkness of night. But he is not there.

The weekend that followed, I could think of nothing but him. I couldn't even tell Susan about it. By the time I got home on Saturday, she'd gone out for the day with Scott. I went to bed and stayed there for the rest of the weekend. I didn't sleep, I didn't eat. I just closed my eyes and focused on his face, remembering every detail of his body, recalling every word of our conversation, every moment of our time together.

I couldn't bear the concept of never seeing him again. I had to find him.

Monday morning, instead of going to work, I went straight to HMV and waited around until they opened. I asked several staff members about the blue-eyed boy, but since I did not know his name they didn't know who I was talking about. Eventually I talked to the store manager, who told me that it was probably the boy who had been doing casual labour for them for the last couple of weeks. He said that he wasn't working there any more. He'd only been there temporarily, and they didn't need him any more. I asked him for the boy's name. The manager didn't want to give it to me, but I kept at him until eventually he checked the payroll records and gave me a name and address.

I wrote the address down and went to Brixton to find my boy. The road existed, but the number didn't. There was no number 138 – the last building on the road was a newsagent's, number 128. I went in there and asked anyway, but no one in there knew the name on the piece of paper. I tried describing the boy, but still no one had seen him.

So I checked number 138 in the next road along, and the next one after that. Eventually I had to accept that the address the boy had given his employers was fake. I assumed the name I had been given was fake, as well. Clearly he did not want to be found. I couldn't imagine what it was he was trying to hide. It was almost as if he had never existed.

Occasionally the thought crosses my mind I dreamed it all, but I know I didn't. The memory, the feelings, are too intense for it to have not been real.

I can't accept he's vanished from my life forever. I've been staying in bed all day and walking the streets of London by night, searching. But he could be anywhere now.

I forgot to ring in sick after that first Friday. Susan came in to my room some time the following week. Wednesday, or Thursday, maybe. I can't remember. I was still in bed.

"There's a letter for you," she said. "It looks like it's from your work."

"I'll open it later," I said from beneath the covers.

"Shelley, your boss phoned yesterday, when I was home on my day off. He asked when you're coming back to work."

"Tell him I'm sick."

"I did. But he says he needs to speak to you about it. Have you been phoning in sick?"

"I'm sick," I repeated.

"So you say," Susan said doubtfully. "What's wrong with you, exactly?"

"Leave me alone and let me sleep. I'm sick."

"You need to phone work, Shelley. You'll get sacked."

I heard Susan leave the room, and close the door behind her. I snuggled up into my duvet some more and went back to sleep. When I woke up again, I got up to use the loo, and noticed Susan had left the envelope on the edge of my bed. I picked it up and threw it in the bin without reading it. Then I went back to bed.

A couple of days ago I was arrested walking down Shaftesbury Avenue, some time late at night. They told me I was walking down the middle of the road, and almost got hit by traffic. I hadn't noticed. I saw those blue eyes in front of me – huge they were, filling the sky. I thought they would lead me to the boy, so I was following them. I guess I wasn't watching where I was going. I don't actually remember how I got to Shaftesbury Avenue. But that's where they told me I was when they found me, so I guess I must have got there somehow.

I must have forgotten to get dressed as well, because when I got to the police station I noticed I was wearing only a short cotton nightie. I was also leaving a trail of bloody footprints across the floor of the police station. They had to get a cleaner to clean up the mess.

I did say I was sorry for making a mess. How did I come to cut my feet? Did I step on some glass? It didn't hurt.

The pain of longing for the blue-eyed boy does hurt, though. Every fibre of my being aches. It will not stop until I find the boy. I must find the boy. The pain will not go away unless I do.

They brought me some clothes and a pair of shoes to wear before bringing me here. A grey tracksuit and trainers. The trainers fit okay, the tracksuit's a bit big, but I guess they didn't know my size.

I don't know how long they are going to keep me here. I keep trying to tell them I don't belong here, but they won't listen.

There are lots of nurses who stalk around in crisp white uniforms. They shove food at me and keep trying to give me injections, but they don't listen.

For a while I tried to fight off the injections, but they started tying me down and giving me more. So now I just let them do it.

I'm not crazy. I'm just in love. If only I were to find my lover, everything would be alright again, and they would let me go home.

I still can't sleep. I lie awake at night seeing his eyes in my mind. Those beautiful, crystal blue eyes.

Does he know how much I need him? He mustn't do, or he would come back, wouldn't he? He would explain that we are lovers, that I'm not crazy, that I don't belong here.

I've got to find him. They won't let me out until I do.

But I can't find him while I'm in here.

And still I don't even know his name.

# Just Don't Scream

Jesse wandered aimlessly through the deserted fairground, the chill wind tousling his dark hair. His good looks were marred by the hard expression and cold eyes of one who is unhappy with life. He stared at his feet as he moved along slowly, kicking at the abandoned sweet wrappers and crisp packets that littered the patchy grass.

As he passed by one of the many red-and-white striped tattered marquees, he thought he heard a voice. He stopped dead and turned to see a small, plump man wearing a huge top hat, peering out from within the folds of the tent.

"Hey," the man said to Jesse. "Come here."

Jesse peered at the man suspiciously. "Why?"

"To play a little game." The man opened the folds of the tent and beckoned Jesse inside. "A guessing game, perhaps. I begin by guessing what you're doing here, and what I can do for you."

"I'm not interested." Jesse turned away and resumed walking.

"For starters," the man called after him, "you're walking around with a face like a wet weekend because your unfaithful girlfriend has ditched you once again. And you've just been made redundant. Correct?"

Jesse hesitated and then looked back at the man, a frown beginning to appear on his face.

The man smiled confidently. "Lucky guess, you think? All right then. I also know your name is Jesse, and that you live in a rundown flat two blocks away from here. And I will tell you that very shortly the opportunity of earning one thousand very easy pounds will come your way."

"I'm impressed," Jesse said reluctantly. "What are you, some kind of psychic?"

"A magician, actually. I have a show here at the fair. Simple, cheap tricks, really, no challenge at all and no real magic involved, but it's what the people pay to see. However, I am now offering you a chance to leave here a thousand pounds richer. No trickery involved."

"How?" asked Jesse, even more suspicious.

"Follow me," said the magician and, with a twinkle in his eye and a mischievous smile on his face, he disappeared into the tent. Intrigued, Jesse went after him.

The magician led the younger man into a curtained-off back area, cluttered with trunks, black boxes, cages of pigeons, gold hoops, brightly-coloured handkerchiefs and other magic paraphernalia. In the centre of the clutter stood a large guillotine, old-looking, but very well cared for. The wood was carefully varnished, and the blade gleamed and shone.

The magician stood by the guillotine like a proud father with his first-born son. He stroked the framework tenderly, almost sensually. "This is the magician's guillotine. My favourite trick. Are you familiar with it?"

"I think so. You stick in a couple of carrots and somebody's head, right? The carrots get cut in half but the person comes out in one piece."

"My trick is a variation, but the same idea," the magician said. "The problem is that people are so squeamish. They hear the blade come down and they scream. It's most frustrating." He sighed.

"So what does this have to do with me?" Jesse asked.

The magician flashed him a peculiar smile. "Well, you see, Jesse, I have a bargain to strike with you." He produced a small metal box from a nearby cupboard and opened it up, pulling out a sheaf of cash. "There is a thousand pounds exactly here. If you can assist me with this trick without screaming, it's yours."

Jesse raised his eyebrows. "What else do I have to do?"

"You're not convinced, are you?" The magician sighed again. "I am a man of my word, Jesse, but like all people I have a couple of peculiar quirks. I have been saving this money strictly for this purpose. I haven't found a soul yet who will keep quiet when the blade comes down. Now you, you look like a brave young fellow. All you have to do is put your head in this groove here, and let me perform the trick, and the money is yours. Just don't scream."

Jesse eyed the magician critically. "I don't believe people give money away just like that. Not if it's that easy. There's got to be a catch."

The magician chuckled. "There's no catch, my friend. However, to convince you, I will have my assistant help me with the trick first to demonstrate how easy it is. Mary Lou!"

Jesse turned sharply. A pretty blonde girl had suddenly materialised in the doorway. She stepped calmly over to stand beside the guillotine, the blood-red cloak over her slim shoulders billowing out behind her. Beneath the cloak she wore a sequined bikini, and elbow-length silk gloves. A black velvet choker encircled her neck.

"Mary Lou has performed this trick countless times," the magician explained, as the girl knelt behind the guillotine and positioned her neck in the groove.

"So give *her* the money."

"Well now, that really wouldn't be fair," the magician replied. "Mary Lou is mute, you see. She is incapable of screaming." He closed the top hinge over the girl's neck, fastened it, and pulled on the rope hanging down the side of the guillotine.

The blade slammed down. Mary Lou flinched slightly, but smiled up at Jesse sweetly as the magician bent to release her. She arose, rubbing her neck and moving her head back and forth as if to demonstrate that it was still attached.

"As you can see, there's nothing to it." The magician kept hold of the hinged bar and gestured at the groove invitingly. "A thousand pounds, my friend. Just waiting for you."

"No hitch?"

The magician shook his head. "No hitch. Just don't scream."

Jesse hesitated a moment longer. He looked at the guillotine; with the bar held up, it almost seemed to be beckoning to him. Then he looked at Mary Lou, standing quietly in front of him, smiling prettily. He walked around behind the guillotine and got to his knees. "What the hell," he muttered to himself."

The magician fastened the bar around Jesse's neck. "Just relax. Look at Mary Lou. You'll come out no worse than she did, I guarantee it."

Jesse looked at Mary Lou, striking up a suggestive model-like pose before him. With a daring half-smile on her lips, she began stripping off her gloves, teasingly, sensuously. From the corner of his eye Jesse saw the magician take hold of the rope. "Remember now, Jesse. Don't scream."

Her gloves off now, Mary Lou was toying with the black choker around her neck. Jesse suddenly felt afraid. Something was wrong, horribly wrong. He opened his mouth to tell the magician to stop, to let him go, he'd changed his mind. At that moment, Mary Lou removed the choker. Her head dropped to the floor and rolled away. Her body remained rigid, and the scarlet cape became a sea of blood flowing down her back.

Jesse screamed.

The blade came crashing down.

The magician, still smiling, picked up the fat pile of money and put it back into the box, closing the lid with triumphant finality. Then he crouched by the severed head on the floor, studying the sightless eyes frozen in terror, the scream that was forever locked on Jesse's face. "You lose," he chuckled softly.

# Cigarette Burns

Kelly pushed herself into the corner of the tube station entranceway, trying to shield herself from the rain, shaking fingers fumbling for the cigarette packet in the breast pocket of her denim jacket.

Shivering from the cold she stuck a cigarette between her lips, taking care to keep it as far to the right side of her mouth as possible. Her lips were still swollen on the left side, tender to the touch. She scrabbled for a match and found one, cupping her hands around the meagre flame to light the cigarette. She took a couple of deep drags and leaned back, trying to calm herself. Her hand shook as she held the cigarette, though whether it was from cold or anger, she no longer knew. She could feel her heart thudding furiously in her chest, and her wet hair hung in limp blonde strands around her shoulders. The bruised and tender flesh around her right eye still stung from the assault of the wind and rain.

She looked back through the doorway at the station foyer, but there was no one around. Scott evidently hadn't arrived yet. At least there was no guard around, to hassle her about loitering. She felt like shit.

She finished her smoke and threw the butt on the floor, feeling at least a little calmer. A moment later, Scott came out of the station. "Hey, Kel. You okay?"

Kelly turned her pale face towards him. "Not really."

Scott's smile of greeting turned into a frown as he came close enough to study her bruised face. "Did he do that to you? Jesus Christ."

"Let's just get out of here," Kelly said. "Can we go for a coffee or something? I'm freezing."

"No problem." Scott took her arm and they headed back into the freezing rain.

They went up the road to McDonald's. The rain was easing off by the time Scott finished chomping his cheeseburger. "You sure you don't want anything to eat?" he asked.

"I'm not hungry." The coffee had helped Kelly thaw out somewhat; her fingertips were still tingling as her nerve endings defrosted. She stared dimly out of the window.

Scott rolled the straw around in the rest of his chocolate shake for a moment, then he looked up at her. "Why don't you come to my place tonight?"

Kelly shook her head. "I'm in shit as it is for going out again. I've got to go back. But I'm scared as hell."

"I'll walk you back."

Kelly sighed. After a moment she got to her feet, turning towards Scott with a sad, haunted look in her red-rimmed eyes. "I guess we should do it, then."

*

Kelly was silent for most of the trek back to her house. "Hey, Kel," Scott said suddenly, slowing beneath a street light. "Look what I got." He showed her the switchblade he had in his pocket.

She looked at it for a minute, blowing smoke into the air. "Where'd you get it?"

"My brother. He knows a guy who gets 'em all the time."

Kelly merely nodded and continued walking. She reached for another cigarette even as she threw the last butt to the ground. She had been chain-smoking ever since they left McDonald's.

Scott hurried to keep up with her, laying a hand on her shoulder. "Hey, take it easy."

"How can I take it easy," she snapped, spinning around, "with what that bastard's been doing to me all my life?" She pulled the cigarette out of her mouth, wincing. "It even hurts to have a smoke because of him." She stuck the cigarette carefully in the right side of her mouth and struck a match. "I hate him, Scott. Even if he is my dad, I hate him so much."

She could feel Scott's eyes on her as she paused to light the cigarette. She was acutely conscious of the marks on her wrists and arms as she brought her hands up to her face, the scars of old cigarette burns.

"It's going to end," Scott said. "Just remember that."

"When I think of what he's done to me." Kelly wasn't listening to him; she was lost in her own world of pain. "How much he's hurt me. I wish I could make him pay for that. For all the pain." She was shaking again.

Scott put his arm around her. "He will pay," he said softly.

They had reached Kelly's street, a long, straight row of Victorian terraces. She hated living here. Grubby kids with snotty noses ran around outside all day while their mothers threw pans at slobby, drunken husbands. There had to be a way out. She and Scott had talked about it so many times. What they would do when they could escape from this shit hole.

"We'll go in through the back." Kelly led Scott down a rubbish cluttered alleyway and through a back gate. A patch of bristly grass and a shed that was falling to bits made up the back garden. Kelly fumbled for her keys and unlocked the back door. Gingerly she pushed it open. She turned to Scott, her fingers to her lips. Then she entered the house.

Scott followed her into the kitchen, where counters were piled high with unwashed dishes and empty beer cans. The room reeked of stale grease.

Kelly hesitated, her hand on the door, and glanced back at Scott.

"What's wrong, Kel?"

"Wait here," she whispered.

"What for?"

"Just let me talk to him. Wait here." Kelly pushed the kitchen door open.

Her father was watching TV. The top of his balding head peeked out from above the back of the sofa. The room was musty with the odours of stale sweat and food.

"That you, Kel?"

"Yes, Dad."

"C'mere."

Kelly paused. Slowly she walked around the sofa to face her father. He looked very much the way he had when she saw him earlier, shirt sleeves rolled up to his elbows, unshaven, a cigarette in his hand. On the stained coffee table in front of him was piled the remains of a meal: dirty plate and cutlery, a ketchup bottle, a couple of empty beer cans, an ashtray overflowing with cigarette butts.

He turned to look at her, his face twisting into a snarl. "Where you been then? You stormed outta here without so much as a by-your-leave. You know I like you to tell me where you're goin'."

"You hurt me, Dad," Kelly said nervously. "I was upset."

"You've been stealin' my fags."

"Only one. I had none. I'll pay you back. I went and bought some." Kelly fumbled in her pocket for the cigarette pack; her hand was shaking. As she offered it to him, something fell out and landed on the floor.

"What's this?" Her father leaned down and picked up the small square of foiled paper. He stared at it for a moment in disbelief. Kelly felt her heart miss a beat. *Oh shit. I'm in for it now.*

"It's a fucking condom." Her father stared at her, his face turning beet red. "What the hell are you doing with this?"

"It isn't mine, Dad, I swear. Sharon gave it to me. I wasn't gonna use it."

"You little slut!" He grabbed her by the arm. "You gonna tell me who you were with tonight?"

Kelly struggled. "No one. I just went out for a walk. I swear."

He caught hold of her hair and pulled her head back. "Don't lie to me. Who were you with?"

"I wasn't with anyone, Dad. Let me go, please."

"You're lyin' to me, Kelly." He slapped her across the face.

Kelly threw her hands to her face, and kicked out blindly, catching her father in the shins.

"You little bitch!" he yelled, and dropped her to the floor. She fell, hitting her head on the corner of the coffee table. Groggily, she tried to claw her way up, hanging on to the side of the table. She reached out for the glass ketchup bottle as her father came down on her. Straddling her, he grabbed her by the collar and hauled her off the floor.

"Tell me who you were with?"

"Nobody."

"Tell me!" He slammed her head down onto the table, scattering the clutter on it. Pain lanced through Kelly's skull and a red haze swam before her eyes. She screamed, and her father lifted her up to slam her down once again. In a panic she swung the bottle and bashed it against the top of his head, so hard the glass broke. Ketchup and glass flew everywhere. Her father howled and let her go. Kelly hit the floor clutching the broken bottle by the neck. Her father swayed on his knees before her, ketchup dripping all down his face. Or was it blood? She saw him making a grab for her again; she tried to get up but her head hurt too much.

She could dimly hear her father yelling, and Scott calling her name. She struggled to lift her head. She saw her father falling back onto the sofa. Scott jumped on him, the switchblade in his hand, plunging it over and over again into her father's chest. Scott's face was red with rage, and he was screaming something unintelligible. Her father was screaming too.

"No, no, stop!" Kelly screamed. "Scott, stop!" There was blood everywhere – all over the floor, the table, the sofa, all over Scott, all over her father.

The screaming stopped. Kelly could hear the blare of the television, but it seemed distant, like a far away dream trying to intrude on a thick blanket of silent slumber. She dropped the broken bottle. It hit the carpet with a dull thud. She stared at her hands, smeared with blood, then at Scott. She felt numb.

"It's finished, Kelly," he said quietly. "He won't hit you again."

Kelly got to her knees. It was done, Scott said, but she was still shaking. Why couldn't she ever stop shaking?

Her father lay sprawled on the sofa, eyes wide and staring, mouth hanging open. The front of his shirt torn and sodden with blood.

Scott looked down at the blood stained blade in his hand. "I want you to go upstairs and pack your stuff," he said. "Take what you need. You won't be coming back here again. Quickly now."

Kelly struggled to her feet and staggered upstairs. Her room felt so safely familiar – it would have been so easy to shut herself away in here and pretend nothing had happened.

From the dressing table mirror a gaunt, white faced girl stared back at her, hair matted with blood, black eyed and bloody lipped. Her head was pounding.

She stumbled downstairs a few minutes later, dragging a sports bag behind her. She didn't know what was in it; she'd stuffed it with whatever came to hand. Her hair was wet; her face raw and sore from trying to scrub all the blood away.

She didn't look towards her father. She didn't want to see. The TV had been turned up; the noise was deafening. As Scott ushered her out of the house, she looked at him. He had washed the blood off his hands and face and he carried his jacket under his arm.

"We killed him, Scott," Kelly mumbled numbly. "We'll go to jail."

Scott squeezed her hand. "Nobody's gonna know what happened, Kel. Nobody's gonna put you in jail. Besides, it was self-defence. He would have killed you. Now he can't hurt you any more."

Kelly let Scott steer her down the street. "Where are we going?"

"Back to my house."

"But what about tomorrow? What about your parents?"

Scott paused to look at her. "Don't worry about that." He smiled then. Kelly looked into his eyes and what she saw there suddenly filled her with terror. "I've already taken care of them."

# The Guitar

The woman sitting at the bar checked her watch for the fifteenth time. Ten-thirty. Well, he just wasn't coming now, simple as that.

Jocelyn was an attractive woman of thirty, tall and slender with a mane of brown curly hair and the sort of legs that could appear in tights advertisements, but the air of hostility she was emitting was enough to convince any man thinking about approaching her to change his mind and walk away.

As a rule, she hated night clubs, and was cursing herself for bad judgement once more – for not only agreeing to go out again with Rick, who had stood her up, but arranging to meet him in this dump. She told herself that she should learn to listen to that small voice inside that had warned her that Rick was a rat, instead of giving in to lust. It wasn't the first time it had happened, and she was angry with herself for making the same mistake again.

She surveyed the dim room distastefully. The air smelled of stale sweat and warm beer. The dance floor was packed, spotlights shining down from the ceiling to illuminate the figures there – girls with no bras, in tight black dresses, and pot-bellied men with a week's worth of stubble and thinning, greasy hair, gyrating to the deafening din of the third-rate rock band on the stage.

She could just make out the band through the swirling smoke of the dry ice blown out through the contraptions rigged up around the dance floor. There were five members, obtusely untalented, unimaginative, and far too loud. The lead singer was about forty. He had glasses and a tangled beard, and his eyes were glassy and unfocussed. He was clearly high on something. He couldn't sing, either. In fact, the only one who seemed to have any ounce of talent was the guitarist, who stood apart from the rest, playing his part and trying to look like he had nothing to do with the others. Now he was pretty good, and he looked out of place compared to the rest of the grizzled band. He was young, blonde and clean-shaven. Even from a distance, Jocelyn thought he looked cute.

She gazed unenthusiastically at the half-pint glass of lukewarm lager in front of her, and thought that she may as well just go home.

But an unreasonably stubborn part of her insisted that that would be admitting defeat. Letting Rick get the better of her, confessing to being stood up on a Saturday night. She didn't relish the prospect of another night alone. She had Sandy to go home to, of course, who was soft and warm to cuddle up to, but Sandy was her neutered ginger tom cat and though he was frequently better company than the men she dated, tonight she was craving human companionship.

She sat up on the bar stool and crossed her legs, tugging on the hem of her leather mini skirt. She would at least finish her drink.

The band was finishing their set. *Thank God that racket's about to stop*, she thought. Turning back to her drink, she noticed a man at the bar looking her up and down. He was about forty, with a thick black moustache. The smile he gave her was more a grimace. *Creep*. Jocelyn glared at him, and purposefully turned away.

Canned pop tunes had started playing to replace the band, but the dance floor was packed with snogging couples nonetheless. It didn't really matter what music was playing at this time of the evening – people were too drunk and too horny to care. Jocelyn scanned the crowded tables bordering the edge of the dance floor, all littered with dirty glasses. A group of about ten women squeezed around one table. Judging from the volume of the raucous laughter, it was probably a hen party. Two couples sat at another table, each couple wrapped up in each other, virtually undressing each other in their eagerness to get down to business. At one of the far tables in the corner, a young man sat alone. Jocelyn gazed at him, and recognised him as the cute guitarist from the band. He sat timidly, both hands wrapped tightly around his pint of beer. His eyes caught hers, and paused.

Jocelyn looked away. She felt other eyes on her, and turned around. Old moustache-face was still leering at her; she could tell from the look on his ogling face that he was ready to make his move. And he looked like the kind of pain-in-the-arse who was impossible to shake.

Making her decision, Jocelyn gathered her handbag and jacket, and walked away from the bar. She carried her glass over to the table in the corner. The young man looked up at her, startled, as she leaned over the table.

"Do you mind if I join you?" she asked, and the sound of her own voice speaking that tired old chat-up line almost made her laugh aloud. *What was she doing?*

The young man shook his head rapidly, wide-eyed. Jocelyn deposited her belongings on the table and sat opposite him.

"Thanks. You know, you sounded pretty good up there."

"Really? I thought it was pretty crappy, myself."

"You were terrific. The rest of the band, however, are terrible."

He grimaced. "Tell me about it. This is my first gig with them. Hopefully it'll be my last."

"How'd an ace guitarist like you get stuck with a band like that, anyway?"

He shrugged. "Paying gigs are hard to find."

"So, what's your name?"

"Mark. What's yours?"

"Jocelyn. Don't laugh," she added as he smiled. "I think my mother must have studied the baby name book, and latched onto it."

"I think it's a lovely name."

"Thank you. So, Mark, can I get you a drink?" *There you go, another cheap chat-up line*, she chided herself. *What's the matter with you?*

"I'll get them," he said. "What are you drinking?"

Jocelyn glanced at her glass of tasteless lager. "I'll have a vodka and tonic." She watched Mark as he made his way to the bar and appreciated the view.

A few minutes later he was back, smiling shyly as he handed over her drink. He seemed embarrassed by her attention, leading her to conclude that he hadn't had a lot of experience with women. And he was very young, no older than twenty. But there was something appealing about his naivety; his pale complexion, dishevelled blond hair and long eyelashes giving him a vulnerable and heartbreakingly sweet appearance that touched something somewhere deep inside her. She drummed her long fingernails on the table thoughtfully.

"What's the matter?" Mark asked.

"Nothing. I was just thinking."

"Oh. What about?"

She smiled. "Nothing important. So, how long have you been playing the guitar?"

"I first picked up a guitar when I was just a kid. About ten years ago. I've been playing ever since. But professionally, only a few months. I was unemployed, so I worked hard at making a career out of music. There's no money in it, though. I don't support myself as a musician; I still live with my parents. It's more for the thrill of playing that I do it. The guitar in my hands becomes a living, breathing being when I play; I can feel her pulse, feel the power flowing through her, enveloping me. She takes over me, she possesses me."

"That's very good," said Jocelyn dryly. "You could take up poetry as well." Mark missed the sarcasm. He was lost in his own world of music. "Have you got another set tonight?"

"Eh?" Mark blinked at her, startled out of his thoughts. "Oh. No, we're done. I was just trying to hide away from the rest of the band. They really are slobs. They were supposed to be arranging digs for us tonight, but I don't think I could face sleeping anywhere they'd picked out."

"Are you going to go home, then?"

"My parents are in Liverpool; it's too far to go tonight. Besides, there's supposed to be another gig tomorrow night. I suppose I should go; I've committed myself. I just don't know if I can take another dive like this."

"So what are you going to do tonight?"

"I guess I'll find somewhere. If worst comes to worst, I can always sleep in my car. I've done it before." He was squinting into the dark club, past Jocelyn's shoulder. She automatically looked behind her, but saw nothing besides masses of sweaty bodies pressed close together. "What's up?" she asked.

"I think that was Roddy – our bassist – leaving. With some girl on his arm. I saw a couple of the other guys leave earlier. Looks like the hotel arrangements have just gone out the window. They could have at least bothered to check to make sure I was going to be okay for the night. Looks like they've left me to fend for myself."

Jocelyn leaned forward to put her empty glass on the table, offering Mark a flash of her generous cleavage. "You could come back to my place for the night."

He blinked, clearly surprised, then grinned broadly. "Sure. Why not?"

"Is your car outside?"

"Yes."

"Then why don't we get out of here now?"

"Let me get my stuff from the back. Wait right here. I won't be a minute." He headed off, a little too quickly. Jocelyn couldn't help but smile at his enthusiasm. He was trying hard to look like he was used to being picked up in night clubs.

He was back in less than five minutes, with a canvas carry-all slung over his shoulder. He had a black guitar case in one hand, and his gig amplifier in the other. "Let's go," he said cheerfully. Jocelyn smiled and followed Mark as he led the way to a battered red Ford Astra in the club's parking lot.

After the sweltering heat of the club it felt all the more cold outside. Jocelyn could see her breath crystallising in front of her. She shivered, pulling her leather jacket closer about her. Her bare legs were coming up in goose pimples. Mark opened the passenger door for her.

Jocelyn had never found a car that could comfortably accommodate her very long legs. She fumbled around beneath the seat and found the handle, pushing the seat back as far as it would go. She arranged herself in the seat and put on her seat belt as Mark deposited his amp and carry-all in the boot, and laid his guitar out carefully on the back seat.

As Jocelyn directed Mark to her flat, he chatted merrily. He talked about nothing but his guitar and his music, and appeared to be completely disinterested in whether or not she was actually listening. Since meeting him, Jocelyn had been wondering why such a good-looking young man had not had a string of girlfriends – and it was quite clear to her that he hadn't. Now she was starting to understand why other women had lost interest. She was already getting bored of his endless monologue; he clearly had no other interests in his life besides music. She kept up her interest in him by imagining him naked, in her bed.

They parked on the road outside Jocelyn's home. The street consisted mainly of large houses that had been divided into flats; Jocelyn's was on the ground floor of number thirty-two, one room with a separate kitchen and bathroom.

Mark turned off the engine and sat looking at the house for a moment.

"Well, let's go in," Jocelyn said. "It's freezing sitting out here."

He looked over at her. "Is it okay if I bring all my stuff in? I don't want to leave it in the car."

"Fine." She left him to lock up the car and went to open the front door.

The corridor was silent and dark, and Jocelyn automatically moved quietly. She often came in late, when everyone else in the house was in bed. Mark crept along as well, struggling with his bag, his guitar and his amp.

She opened the door of her flat, and Mark followed her in. She flicked on the light. "Make yourself at home," she said as she closed and bolted the door.

"Thanks," Mark said nervously. She saw him looking around the room; trying to see it from his eyes. It was spacious enough for a bedsit. A wardrobe and drawer unit covered one wall, with a full-length mirror on one of the wardrobe doors. The furniture was modern, all black and red: a table, two chairs, a large double bed, bookshelves, stereo and TV unit. Mark carefully set his amp down on the floor and deposited his bag on the table. He stood looking around uncertainly, his guitar case in hand.

"Sit down," said Jocelyn. "Would you like some coffee?"

"That'd be great, thanks."

"Okay then. I'll be right back." She went into the kitchen and switched on the light. Sandy the cat blinked at her sleepily from his place on the window sill.

"Go back to sleep, you great lump," Jocelyn said affectionately.

She filled the kettle and plugged it in. She hummed to herself as she clattered around the kitchen gathering mugs, spoons and coffee. She poked her head around the kitchen door. Mark had plugged his amp into the wall socket and was softly strumming his guitar. "Milk and sugar?" Jocelyn asked.

Mark stopped playing, flicking his hair out of his eyes as he raised his head. "Yes, please. Two sugars."

"Right." She retreated into the kitchen, and spooned coffee into each of the two mugs. She wondered why she was going through the charade of coy seduction. *Serving coffee, indeed. Why not just accost him now and have done with it?*

As she opened the fridge door to get the milk, Sandy became animated. He stepped down onto the counter and walked across it, then jumped to the floor, stopping by his dish and looking up at her expectantly. "No fooling you, is there, cat?" She bent down to pour milk into the dish.

As she put the milk on the counter, the boiling kettle switched itself off. She yanked on the lead of the kettle to pull the plug out of the socket. As she did so, there was a bang and a flash, and a sharp pain coursed up her arm.

Jocelyn put the kettle down hastily and leapt away from it. She rubbed her arm, but the tingling sensation was already fading; mild electric shock, perhaps, but no serious damage. *Had a fuse blown?* She stared at the socket. It wasn't smouldering, and there was no sign of any scorch marks. The light was on and the fridge was still humming in its corner of the kitchen, so the rest of the electrics in the room appeared to be fine.

She poked at the kettle gingerly. Nothing happened. She picked it up. Still nothing.

She finished making the coffee, and carried it into the other room. She put Mark's mug down on the table.

"Thanks," he said. He was picking out a tune that sounded vaguely familiar to her. She sat on the bed and drank her coffee.

"Sometimes it seems like a magical instrument, the guitar," Mark said quietly. "It alternates between soft, beautiful sounds and raucous, dissonant ones. I often feel that the sound of the music doesn't represent the skill of the player, but the personality of the guitar. She's a fickle creature, of many moods, sometimes soft and seductive, sometimes cruel."

"You talk about it as if it's a person."

"She is a person. To me, anyway. To me it's like she has a mind of her own."

Jocelyn watched his long delicate fingers touch the strings, as tenderly as a lover. She felt a twinge of unreasonable jealousy, aware of Mark's attention being solely on the guitar, attention that she desired. *Jealous of a guitar? Don't be so silly*, she scolded herself.

"Come and sit over here with me," she said. "You'll be much more comfortable."

Mark looked at her. He stood up and propped the guitar carefully on the chair. Slowly, he approached the bed. He stopped as he reached her and remained standing. Jocelyn smiled, and took both his hands in hers, guiding him down gently to her. He lay beside her and she took his face in her hands. His eyes were a clear, pale blue, his eyelashes as long as a young girl's. Then she kissed him tenderly.

He responded, tentatively at first, but then starting to relax. When they separated, he lay back, his face flushed. "I – I think there's something I should tell you before we go any further," he stammered.

"Are you a virgin, Mark?"

"It's that obvious, is it?" He sounded dismayed.

She smiled. "Don't worry about it. I'm flattered. I have to say it's pretty unusual, though."

"It's just that I was always shy around girls. Most of them don't seem to be too interested in music. I guess I've never been able to make anyone else understand how important it is to me."

"That doesn't matter now." Jocelyn drew him closer to kiss him again.

A vicious hiss made them both start, and Mark leapt up as if he'd been stung. Jocelyn sat up. Sandy was standing in the kitchen doorway, his body rigid, his fur standing on end. His eyes flashed and he hissed again, his hostility directed, it seemed to Jocelyn, at the guitar.

"Sandy, what's got into you?" she snapped, irritated.

"Cats normally like me," Mark said.

"I don't think it's you." Jocelyn lunged at the cat. "Get out of here, you stupid animal."

Sandy turned and scurried back into the kitchen. A moment later, the cat-flap on the back door banged. Jocelyn, feeling uneasy, went back to the bed.

"He's never done that before. I think it was your guitar he didn't like." She gazed suspiciously at the instrument. It sat there, perfectly harmless, black polished surface gleaming in the light.

"If he's never seen one before, perhaps that's why it scared him."

"Perhaps." Jocelyn sighed. She looked at Mark, who stood pressed up against the door. "I wish you'd relax, Mark. I promise I'll be gentle." She grinned.

Mark smiled and went to her. They embraced on the bed. She ran her hand through his silky hair, down his neck, across his back. He trembled beneath her touch.

She pulled away. "What are you so frightened of?"

"I can't help it," he said nervously. "I'm sorry."

"Would it help if we turned off the light?"

"It might."

She flicked the light switch. The light of a lone street lamp outside the window filtered in, reflecting dark shapes and shadows in the room. Mark sat, silhouetted, on the bed. The guitar a black mass on the chair beside it.

In the darkness they undressed. Mark fumbled with the zip of his jeans for a long time; when he finally got them off he tossed them hastily to the floor. Jocelyn heard the rustle of his clothes, then the creak of the springs as he got into bed beside her.

He reached out to touch her, and his hands were cool. She drew him closer to her, enveloping him in her warm body, and wrapped her legs around him. She kissed him again, her hands exploring his naked flesh. He moved his hands down to tentatively touch her breasts.

Excited now, his kisses were more confident. His touch was gentle; he ran his hands through Jocelyn's hair, entangling his fingers in its luxurious thickness. He scrambled on top of her, clumsy in his eagerness, his body pressed heavily against hers. As he entered her he emitted a cry, as if in pain, a sound that betrayed an onrush of emotions and sensations.

The overhead light suddenly snapped on, dazzling Jocelyn. Mark gave a cry of surprise and withdrew, rolling off her. Squinting, shielding her eyes against the glare of the light, Jocelyn sat up. "What the hell ...?" she muttered.

She scanned the room but there was nothing there. Same old furniture, Mark's bag on the table, two empty mugs, his guitar on the chair, amp on the floor, items of clothing and shoes scattered haphazardly on the carpet. Mark's jeans were draped carelessly across the amp, where they had landed when he had discarded them.

Jocelyn hesitated as she looked at the guitar. There was something foreboding about it, somehow; perhaps the colour, the way the light gleamed off the lacquered surface. The control knobs stared out at her, like eyes ...

Watching her.

Watching her make love to Mark.

Shaking her head to clear it, Jocelyn got out of bed, climbing over Mark who lay huddled under the covers, and went to the light switch. She looked at it closely before touching it; she couldn't understand what had made it come on. The switch was still in the 'off' position. Gingerly she flicked it and stepped back; nothing happened.

"Odd," she said, staring at it. After a moment she flicked the switch again, back to the 'off' position. The light went out.

She stood for a minute in the dark, a cold chill creeping up and down her spine. She remembered the socket in the kitchen. Maybe her whole electrical system was on the blink. Shivering, she hurried back to the warmth of the bed.

"I'm sorry," Mark mumbled. "I wanted to wait a bit longer. I tried, really." He lay with his back to her, curled up in the foetal position.

"It's alright," she said softly. "Really." She reached to embrace him. He turned around and clung to her tightly. It felt strange to Jocelyn to utter such comforting post-coital phrases for she felt like nothing had happened. Nonetheless, her passion had subsided. She still felt a chill, and she held Mark more for comfort than out of desire.

He fell asleep long before she did, still with his arms wrapped around her, like a child clutching a teddy bear. She stroked his hair, needing the reassurance that he was there, needing to touch him, to hold him, but not wanting to wake him.

She felt frightened, inexplicably, and that the darkness around her sheltered something terrifying, and she felt desperately alone. She had never been frightened of the dark before, not even as a child, and she couldn't explain why she was suddenly afraid now. But putting on that light meant getting out of bed to walk through the darkness and, even worse, touching that switch. Eventually, she did fall into a fitful slumber.

When she woke, it was still dark. She glanced at her alarm clock; it was half past three. Mark still slept beside her, but his hold on her had relaxed.

Lying back in the darkness, she gradually became aware of what had awakened her. She could hear a series of chords being strummed, very softly.

She sat up and looked over at the guitar. It was glowing very distinctly, emitting a soft red light. Its strings glinted silver, each one moving gently as the chords played.

"Mark!" Jocelyn hissed in fear. Clutching the sheet in one hand, she prodded him with the other.

"Mmm." Mark mumbled and rolled over. Jocelyn poked him again.

The light blazed on once more, and the strumming abruptly stopped. Jocelyn shielded her eyes. Mark muttered angrily and pulled the covers up over his head. "Whass'the matter?" she heard him say.

"Your guitar," she whispered numbly. "It's glowing." She looked again at the guitar. It wasn't glowing now. It leaned against the chair where Mark had left it.

He poked his head out from beneath the covers, squinting in the light. "What did you say? Why did you turn the light on?"

"I didn't turn it on. It came on by itself. Like before. But before that happened, your guitar was glowing."

Mark looked over at it. Then he looked back at Jocelyn as if she'd gone mad. "Why should it do that?" Mark pulled the sheet back over his head. "Please turn out that light."

"I don't want to touch that damn switch. Not if it's turning itself on and off like that all the time."

Mark said nothing further. Jocelyn nudged him and he didn't stir. "I'm glad somebody can sleep," she muttered sarcastically. There was no reply. She missed having Sandy at the foot of the bed; this was the first time in months he hadn't slept there.

She got out of bed resignedly and went once more to the light switch by the door. Before she had a chance to touch it, the light went out again. Jocelyn backed away from it in fear. She scooped up her satin dressing gown from the chair over which it was draped and wrapped it tightly about herself.

Entering the kitchen, she hesitated for a moment before touching the light switch. The light came on, as normal.

She crouched down by the back door and peered through the cat-flap. It wasn't like Sandy to stay out so long, especially when it was cold. He was a lazy old thing who liked staying warm. She called him a couple of times through the cat-flap, but got no response. Perhaps he was sulking because she'd shouted at him. She thought back to his peculiar reaction earlier; it was not like

Sandy to get hostile.

The kitchen was ominously quiet, and Jocelyn suddenly realised what was missing. The fridge wasn't humming. Mumbling furiously to herself, she opened the refrigerator door. The light inside didn't come on. She peered at the socket; it was still plugged in. The other socket shorting out earlier must have blown a fuse somewhere. She cursed under her breath, and padded across the kitchen floor. Her foot touched something wet, and she looked down to see a trail of blood spots across the linoleum. The blood was running down her leg. What was the date? The fourth. She was early. She wasn't usually early, it had caught her out. Damn, damn, damn.

She hurried into the bathroom and reached for the box of Tampax in the cupboard. She sat on the toilet with her head in her hands. *God, why was everything going wrong tonight?* As if reading her thoughts, the bathroom light flickered off. Had to be a power cut now, or the fuse had blown and shut everything off.

Jocelyn staggered back to the kitchen, which was also now in darkness, and rummaged around under the sink. She had a battery-powered lamp under there. It took a few minutes, but she finally managed to lay her hands on it. She turned it on and took it back to the bathroom, setting it on the side of the bath. The light it shed was dim, but allowed her to see sufficiently. She put the plug in the old stained cast iron bath and turned on the taps. She had to get herself cleaned up, and she wasn't tired anymore. She'd probably stained the sheets as well, but she wasn't going to throw Mark out of bed at three in the morning to change them. Hopefully he wouldn't notice. A boy who had been a virgin till the age of twenty probably didn't know much about menstruation.

As the water ran, she shuffled back into the kitchen and took a towel from the airing cupboard.

An unearthly yowling from behind her nearly sent her leaping out of her skin. She whirled around. Sandy stood in the kitchen doorway, his back to Jocelyn. He stood with his hackles raised, all his fur standing completely on end, looking as if he had stuck a paw into an electric socket.

"God, Sandy, where did you come from?" Jocelyn exclaimed, and then realised that Sandy had barely even noticed her. He was staring at the guitar, oblivious to all else around him. From deep in his throat came a terrible sound, of fear and anguish.

"Sandy ..." she whispered, completely unnerved. She had never heard Sandy make such a sound before, and it was frightening. She stepped forward, intending to scoop him up in her arms, but the cat emitted another terrible growl that made her stop dead in her tracks. She backed slowly into the bathroom.

She turned off the taps, shed her robe and stepped into the bath. She lay back, relishing the comfort of the steaming water. She stared at the grimy and cracked ceiling of her bathroom, dancing with eerie shadows cast by the meagre light of the battery-powered lamp.

She lathered a face cloth with a good helping of Imperial Leather, and ran the suds over her water-slicked skin, thinking how marvellous it was that no matter how bad you felt, a hot bath was always the remedy. Even in the middle of the night, she reflected bitterly, though her fatigue had evaporated.

She did not think there was any point in going back to bed now. What could she do to pass the time till morning? Go for a long walk? Probably not a good idea in this neighbourhood, given the hour. Or she could start looking up numbers of electricians to call in the morning, since that damned blown fuse was causing so many problems.

Lying back in the water, Jocelyn was brought back from her wandering thoughts by a horribly dissonant sound, gradually increasing in crescendo, coming from the living room. She frowned. It sounded like a guitar, but being played by someone who knew absolutely nothing about music. It sounded as if each note was being ripped from the guitar in excruciating pain.

A terrible howling started then – Sandy again, making that piercing, soul-wrenching wailing. Jocelyn heard his claws clattering on the kitchen floor as he thundered across the flat.

The last thought in her head was of her cat, wondering what on earth could be wrong that he was making that terrible sound.

Then Sandy tore into the bathroom and leapt onto the side of the bath, knocking the power lamp into the water where Jocelyn lay.

Electrocution came so quickly, she barely had time to scream.

Even if the scream had been longer, it would not have awoken Mark. He slept on in the next room, drugged by the tender, haunting lullaby that came from the strings of his beloved guitar, the guitar that glowed a soft red in the drowsy darkness.

# Someone To Watch Over You

When I was alive, I often used to wonder what happened to us after we die. I was never religious. My parents both came from Catholic families, but neither was particularly devout. We went to Church at Christmas and Easter; plus for weddings, christenings and funerals. At home nobody really talked religion; my sister and I were left to make our own choices. I never really believed in the idea of Heaven and Hell, but I always believed that there was a part of us that lived on after death; an essence of some kind. The human psyche always seemed, to me, to be far too complex to consist of nothing but flesh and bone.

But, I am getting ahead of myself. I should introduce myself. You should not make the mistake of assuming I am the person who writes these words. She is merely a means to an end. I have no physical form, and the words will not write themselves.

When I was alive, my name was Elizabeth Anne Beresford. I went to university and gained a degree in English; and became successful in business editing a popular women's magazine. I had no husband, no children, no family apart from my sister Bridget. My father died of lung cancer when I was a teenager, my mother died from a brain haemorrhage when I was twenty-four. Bridget was ten years younger than I; we were always very close, and we grew even closer after the death of my mother, when it was left to me to take care of her.

You do not know it yet, but you will have questions for me. To pre-empt the first, I died in a car crash at the age of twenty-eight. It was a cold, wet day in November. I was meeting a client for dinner after a very stressful day, and the trains had been subject to delays all week, so I decided to drive. It was raining hard, the roads were wet, visibility was poor, and I was in a hurry, so I was driving too fast. I was tired, I'd had a hellish week, and I was not looking forward to the meeting. I had thought about cancelling, but decided that would be unprofessional. What sort of business image would I project if I let clients down?

So the evening found me driving through the pouring rain into London, and my concentration was not at its best. I was dazzled by oncoming lights and did not see the car ahead slam on its brakes. When I did it was too late, I swerved, lost control of the car, and hit the wall.

Oh, it was very quick, and completely painless. Death remains one of the greatest fears of human kind, but I can say with complete authority that in my case, at least, there was nothing to fear. It was all over so quickly, it took me a while to realise I was dead.

After the wall came up to meet me, there was a terrible tearing, crunching sound, and the next thing I knew I was looking down on the crumpled remains of my car. In my initial confusion I thought I had been thrown clear, but I could not feel any part of my body, I could not scream, and none of the people running to help seemed to notice me. Only when I saw my mangled body being dragged out of the car did the truth hit me with chilling clarity.

Am I a ghost? That would depend on how you would define ghosts. In physical form I ceased to exist at the moment of the crash. I cannot appear as a shimmering image before people. I exist on a different plane. I have awareness, and in that sense I still perceive myself, I still exist as a thinking, reasoning being, but that awareness is all I am – I am no more than an abstract idea. I can view what goes on in the physical world, but I exist parallel to it, and cannot be heard or touched or seen by anyone on that parallel world.

Those who are particularly sensitive to things that exist beyond the three dimensions of the physical world may be aware of my presence, if I linger nearby, but they cannot define what or who I am – they are merely aware of another presence in the vicinity.

This existence I now know is a lonely one. Once the realisation of my death had sunk in, and I had come to accept it, I attempted to seek out my parents – for, I reasoned, they were dead, too, and therefore must be here somewhere – wherever 'here' was. I soon learned, however, that there are an infinite number of plains of existence for those whose physical body has ceased to exist, which all run parallel and never meet. Every so often a dimension passes close enough to mine for another presence to flicker by – a tiny shimmer of consciousness, just a glimpse of another like myself, but then it is gone forever, never to cross my path again. Never have I felt a presence that defined itself to me as my mother or my father. Heaven and Hell are one to me, existing simultaneously, and I can only observe the world of the living, a painful reminder of what I used to be and can never be again.

Another discovery I have made in this eternal torment of existence is that time is only linear to the living. I can define the passage of time in the physical world by observing my sister; by pinpointing a single moment in her life and noting at what age she appears at that moment, or observing similarly her husband and children, who all came into her life after my death. I am no longer aware of the date, or even the year, in the physical world, for time is everything at once to me. All that is past, present and future is to me instantaneous – I know what is past and what is to come.

Perhaps you want to ask, if I know all the past and all the future, can I change it? No I cannot, which adds to the eternal torment in which I exist. But in all the time I have been in this form, a non-entity with conscious thought, I have discovered how I can influence the physical world.

At the time of my death my sister Bridget was working as a shop assistant in a book shop in London. Every morning she took the train from my parents' house in Clapham Junction to Victoria station, on her way to work.

It was difficult for me, for a long time after my death, to observe my sister's pain and be powerless to ease her grief. For she was alone in the world now, wandering around in the big house my parents had bequeathed to us, with no company except for the five cats we kept as pets. I observed her sitting alone for countless evenings with two or three of the cats on her lap, talking to them as she watched the television. Sometimes she would start talking to me instead. I longed to let her know that I could hear her, that I was still watching over her, even in death. Sometimes I felt she could sense my presence, and gained comfort from it.

Then a terrorist's bomb went off at Victoria station, exploding in a litter bin in front of platform four, killing two people and injuring many more. One of those killed was my sister Bridget, as she got off her train as usual and happened to be passing the litter bin as the bomb exploded. I knew all this, as I know all past and present and future events at once, but I also saw another future for my sister, one in which she married and had children, banished the loneliness from her life and found happiness. I wanted to make sure she could find this happiness, and live.

I visited Bridget the evening preceding the day of the bomb. Everything she did that night, I was watching. She came home from work and lay for a long time in a hot bath, lying beneath the water as the bathroom filled with steam. When she emerged from the bath she put on a night-dress and her pink fluffy dressing gown, and wrapped her blonde hair in a blue towel. She fried herself some chips and grilled a chicken Kiev – the pre-prepared and frozen kind – and ate her dinner while watching television. She went to bed early and read a few chapters of Stephen King's 'Carrie', finally falling asleep with three of the cats snuggled up on the bed with her.

All night I watched Bridget as she slept, thinking of nothing but the fact that she must not go to work in the morning. She had to phone in sick. She must not get on her usual train. It seems I filled the room with these thoughts. I knew I had no power to change things in the living world, but my dread of Bridget boarding that train in the morning became so overpowering I could almost feel it.

My sister slept fitfully that night, and I don't doubt it was a result of the fretful thoughts with which I was filling her bedroom. Just before her alarm rang, at 7.00 am, she awoke, staggered to the bathroom, and vomited down the toilet. She flushed the toilet and sat on the floor for a long time, her arms crossed over her knees, and her forehead resting on her forearms. When she crawled back to bed her alarm was ringing. She switched it off, climbed beneath the covers, and went to sleep.

I was still watching, willing Bridget to be ill. She slept, tossing and turning, and when she woke up again it was 9:15. She got out of bed, pulled her dressing gown about herself, and shuffled to the telephone. She phoned the shop to explain to her boss that she was not feeling well, and would not be coming into work today. It was then that she was told a bomb had exploded at the station, a few minutes after her usual train was due to arrive.

Bridget hung up the phone and stood in the chilly living room for a long time, her arms wrapped around her shoulders, her eyes wide and staring, her face pale.

*You are alive, Bridget,* I thought at her. *I am here, looking out for you. I will not let anything happen to you.*

Bridget went back to bed but could not go back to sleep, and after a while got up and made herself some toast, realising that she felt much better. I had suggested to her that she was not well; somehow this idea was transmitted to her successfully, and she awoke not feeling well. I felt cheered by this, as I realised that I could make a difference to those I cared about – I could not change anything in the physical world, but I could influence the thoughts of those I loved, and protect them in some small way.

I am watching now, not only Bridget but her husband John, and their three children.

I cannot always protect them. I tried my best to suggest to John that he should not climb the ladder outside their house to fix the loose drainpipe on the roof, but he still climbed it, fell off and broke his arm.

I also know there will come a point when I cannot interfere. Bridget must die, as all living beings must, but she is destined now to die peacefully, as an old woman, and when that moment comes I will do nothing but be with her, silently reassuring her that there is nothing to fear.

I know also how, and when, her husband and children will die, but I cannot divulge that – I have given you too much information already. I have told you what death is like – this is more than the living ought to know.

And what of me? Was that car crash my destiny? On reflection I think, perhaps, it was only one of many, as Bridget's death in the Victoria bombing was only one of several possible destinies.

Perhaps I should have listened to that voice in my head the night of my death? The one that told me to cancel the dinner, take the train home and have an early night to wind down after a stressful week. Perhaps that was the voice of my own guardian angel, trying to alter my fate? I shall never know, as I shall never know what my destiny would have been had I remained in the physical world for longer than I did.

So these words you now read come from me, these words I am putting in the mind of a writer whose imagination is responsive to my suggestions.

We are out here, those of us whose love for others carries beyond the grave. We observe, we care, we try to protect. We act as guardian angels for those we cared about in life.

Chances are, you have someone too – someone you loved, who is now gone from the mortal world. You may be familiar with that small voice from somewhere inside you that might some day tell you not to get on that plane, or to cancel that evening out, or to go back to bed instead of struggling into work today.

My message to you now is that when you hear that voice, you should listen to it. That voice you hear may be someone you loved and lost, who even in death is still watching over you.

# Postscripts

**The Thirteenth Floor:** I got the idea for this story when I went to visit someone who lived on the fourteenth floor of an apartment block. I noticed the floors went from twelve to fourteen, and I started to think about what might have happened to the thirteenth floor.

This was one of the first stories I tried submitting for publication. It got picked up very quickly, appearing in the October 1989 issue of FEAR magazine. They paid me £50.00 for it. I was nineteen at the time, and got rather cocky, thinking I was going to get rich from this writing business and there was nothing to it, a misconception I was rapidly disabused of.

Looking back, *The Thirteenth Floor* is perhaps a story with flaws, it being one of my earlier ones, but it was also my first published story and I have a fondness for it for that reason.

**Jimi Hendrix Eyes:** I've always used writing as a way of dealing with painful or difficult emotions. My own fears and insecurities run through my writing as recurring themes. Fear of betrayal pops up a lot, as it does in this story.

It's still painful to read this story, because I was in a rather bad place when I wrote it. But it at least makes me realise how far I've moved on since then.

**Trio:** As a lonely teenager I joined an amateur theatre group, and one of the things I loved about being part of it was that there I could be accepted for who I was. The first production I was involved in was a cheesy family drama called MAXIMILIAN BEETLE, in which all the characters were insects (I played an ant). There were a lot of teens in the cast, and three of us became very good friends. We hung out a lot together, and I came to think of us as The Trio. It was from them I drew inspiration for this story, though the melancholy slant came out of my own imagination – happily my two real-life muses are alive and well and I still count them amongst my good friends. Andrea and Aaron, this one's dedicated to you.

**To Dream of An Angel:** Back in the early 1990s I was part of a writing group, mostly made up of horror writers. They were all very nice people, who wrote really sick stories. Two events inspired this tale, and found their way into it – the conversation about dreams and the vision that Jenny has with the knife are both based on real events. Written in the early days of a new relationship, my own insecurities about loss and abandonment combined with reality to produce this somewhat melancholy, ethereal tale.

I haven't seen him in twenty years, but the character of Dean in this story is based on the chap who hosted those meetings. Scott, if you're out there, thanks for the inspiration.

**Kay's Blues:** I cannot take credit for coining the phrase about period pain being like "having a dwarf swinging from your kidneys". I heard it from a friend of mine, who may even have been relaying it from a friend of hers. But I thought it was such a good phrase I wanted to use it somewhere.

Many women can relate to getting a bit crazy when suffering from PMT. But if you get crazy enough to go into murderous rampages, can you still blame it on hormones? I decided to explore that concept in a story, rather than find out for real.

**The Wedding Hat:** The idea of mysterious shopkeepers selling magical and/or cursed items is a common theme in horror stories. That was the starting point for this tale. I also wanted to explore the concept of whether our fate is fixed, or if we make our own destiny. Alex's obsession with death inevitably leads her to suicide.

**Morgan's Father:** The main character in this story is purposefully named after Morgan Le Fay, the unbalanced witch in the Pendragon legend. I moved out of my comfort zone with this one. It's the only story of mine written in present tense.

**Train To Maladomini:** I have spent many years commuting to London on the train to get to work, and can relate to the concept that the journey is Hell. I decided to take that metaphor a step further, and write a story in which Hell turns out to be a train.

**The Boy With Blue Eyes:** Several years ago my amateur theatre group put on a performance of Tennessee Williams' ORPHEUS DESCENDING. I was intrigued with the main character, a drifter musician. The men view this charismatic stranger in town with fear and suspicion, but he drives the women into a state of all-consuming passion. Thinking about this inspired me to write this story of the devastatingly charming but mysterious blue-eyed boy. People do crazy things in the name of love. What if passion can literally drive a person mad?

**Just Don't Scream:** This was one of my first horror stories, written when I was seventeen. I was an introverted, shy and insecure teenager, who did well in school, didn't go out on dates, and wasn't brave enough to do anything rebellious. Instead I delved into my imagination, and wrote unpleasant stories that would shock people.

I have a particular affection for this story, flaws and all, because I can see how my writing has progressed since I wrote it. And I am still fond of stories with the 'shock' ending.

**Cigarette Burns:** For six years I trekked across London after work to evening classes at the University of North London, studying for my English degree. I had a ten-minute walk from Kentish Town tube station to my campus. I remember it mostly being a cold, dark, and somewhat creepy walk.

The station was generally quiet by the time I got off there, since I arrived after all the commuters had gone. It was during that lonely walk that Kelly came to me – someone vulnerable and fragile, huddling to find shelter in the lonely, unfriendly tube station. Why she was there and what she was waiting for came to me as I began to develop the story. And as I started to tell the tale of Kelly's abusive father, my penchant for twist endings came out once more – what if the boyfriend who's saving her turns out to be even worse?

**The Guitar:** The man I have been with for 22 years plays the guitar, and this is undoubtedly the reason why guitarists feature so often in my writing. In many ways, he and I understand each other because his passion for playing guitar is similar to my passion for writing. But then, inspired by Stephen King's tale of the possessive car, CHRISTINE, I started to think, what would happen if the guitar could get jealous?

**Someone To Watch Over You:** What happens after we die? The concept I was trying to explore with this story is that we live on in some ethereal form, and time ceases to be linear. Some people believe in 'guardian angels'. What if they are people we have loved and lost, trying to watch out for us from their ethereal plane?

This is the only story in the collection that has any kind of happy ending. Although the main character is dead, and is telling the story from beyond the grave, she has found peace in protecting her sister.

It seemed appropriate to finish on that note. I'd like to thank you for staying with me until the end of the ride. I may have taken you to some dark places, but we've both come out the other side, into the light once more.

# Biography – Sara Jayne Townsend

**Sara Jayne Townsend** was born in Cheshire in 1969, and spent most of the 1980s living in Canada after her family emigrated there. She now lives in Surrey with two elderly cats and her guitarist husband Chris. She has been making up stories since childhood, and knew by the age of 10 that she was destined to be a writer.

She co-founded the London-based T Party Writers' Group (http://www.t-party.org.uk) in 1994, and remains Chair Person. She is the author of two published e-books, *Suffer The Children* and *Death Scene*, both of which are available in all e-reader formats from Lyrical Press (www.lyricalpress.com) and most e-book retail websites.

Sara's website can be found at:
www.sarajaynetownsend.weebly.com

## Also from Stumar Press

## Derby Scribes 2011 Anthology

Eleven short stories featuring Simon Clark, Conrad Williams, Neal James and Derby Scribes members including Richard Farren Barber, Stuart Hughes and Christopher Barker.

* "This anthology reminded me that even short fiction can pack a powerful punch." - Dark Side of the Covers.

* "This is a good collection, that showcases some fine talent." - Ginger Nuts of Horror.

* "I can absolutely recommend this anthology." - A Book A Day.

Available from Stumar Press www.stumarpress.co.uk

## Also from Stumar Press

*Spare Parts* - a collection of six short stories from British Fantasy Award Winning author Stuart Young.

"Young serves up six stories on the theme of love and loss, and the quiet desperation of ordinary lives suddenly transformed by accidental magic." – Simon Morden

"Stuart Young not only writes stories, he gives them life." – Tim Lebbon

"Young's writing is never less than rewarding, while at his best he is thought provoking and capable of genuinely moving the reader." – Peter Tennant

"Stuart Young writes like Roald Dahl with a freshly sharpened butcher knife, effortlessly cutting straight to the heart." – Mark McLaughlin

Available from Stumar Press www.stumarpress.co.uk

## Coming Summer 2012 from
## Hersham Horror Books

# ALT-ZOMBIE

The Alternative–Zombie anthology containing even more original short   stories from authors you love to read. Including stories from writers like Joe McKinney, Gary McMahon, Shaun Jeffrey, Stephen Bacon, Dave Jeffery, Mark West, Stuart Hughes, Willie Meikle, Jan Edwards, David Williamson,  Alison Littlewood *and* many, many more ...

http://hershamhorrorbooks.webs.com

www.ingramcontent.com/pod-product-compliance
Lightning Source LLC
Chambersburg PA
CBHW052206170626
46812CB00004B/1677